THREE
STRIKE
SUMMER

THREE STRIKE SUMMER

Skyler Schrempp

Margaret K. McElderry Books   New York London Toronto Sydney New Delhi

MARGARET K. McELDERRY BOOKS
An imprint of Simon & Schuster Children's Publishing Division
1230 Avenue of the Americas, New York, New York 10020

Text © 2022 by Skyler Schrempp
Jacket and interior illustrations © 2022 by Sas Milledge
Jacket design by Greg Stadnyk © 2022 by Simon & Schuster, Inc.
MARGARET K. McELDERRY BOOKS is a trademark of Simon & Schuster, Inc.
For information about special discounts for bulk purchases, please contact Simon & Schuster Special Sales at 1-866-506-1949 or business@simonandschuster.com.
The Simon & Schuster Speakers Bureau can bring authors to your live event. For more information or to book an event, contact the Simon & Schuster Speakers Bureau at 1-866-248-3049 or visit our website at www.simonspeakers.com.
Interior design by Irene Metaxatos
The text for this book was set in ITC Galliard Std.
Manufactured in the United States of America
0722 FFG
First Edition
10 9 8 7 6 5 4 3 2 1
Library of Congress Cataloging-in-Publication Data
Names: Schrempp, Skyler, author.
Title: Three strike summer / Skyler Schrempp.
Description: First edition. | New York : Margaret K. McElderry Books, [2022] | Audience: Ages 8 to 12. | Audience: Grades 4–6. | Summary: "Dust Bowl refugee Gloria Mae Willard finds herself uprooted and working on a California peach orchard, where she tries to join the secret, all-boys baseball team that she's desperate to play on"—Provided by publisher.
Identifiers: LCCN 2021046836 (print) | LCCN 2021046837 (ebook) | ISBN 9781534499140 (hardcover) | ISBN 9781534499164 (ebook)
Subjects: CYAC: Baseball—Fiction. | Agricultural laborers—Fiction. | Migrant labor—Fiction. | Family life—California—Fiction. | California—History—20th century—Fiction. | LCGFT: Novels. | Historical fiction.
Classification: LCC PZ7.1.S336538 Th 2022 (print) | LCC PZ7.1.S336538 (ebook) | DDC [Fic]—dc23
LC record available at https://lccn.loc.gov/2021046836
LC ebook record available at https://lccn.loc.gov/2021046837

To kids in migration.
Here and there.
Then and now.

THREE STRIKE SUMMER

Part One

Chapter One

Outside, just beyond our front door, Pa was having a word with the bank man.

Inside, Jessamyn splashed a cold shock of water over my scalp to loosen up the last week's worth of dust from my hair. It sloshed at the bottom of the washbasin, cloudy as pond muck.

"Watch it you don't splash my eye," I spat, shaking my head like a wet dog.

"What you gotten into anyway? Your head's as dirty as your feet," said Jess.

"Good," I said, "that's how I like it."

Jess answered back with another pour of water that flooded my eyes and ears for just a moment.

She was doing this on purpose. Washing my hair. Keeping my head down. Pinning me here in the kitchen over a doggone washbasin. She was doing it so I wouldn't see what was going on.

But I knew.

I knew that bank man was coming. I knew what he was there for. And I knew what would happen when he was done with us.

Besides, Jess couldn't keep me from peering up through my dripping locks to look down the dark empty hall into the empty sitting room and out there just beyond the screen door.

Pa was standing there, stunted fields of wheat behind him, our sad, still windmill looking on in the distance. He was standing, all dust and jeans and wounded pride. Seeing him like that, his work shirt faded and thin against the black brushed suit of that man, made me hold on tight to the washbasin so the world wouldn't spin too bad.

It'd been spinning a lot more than usual lately.

"Quit looking, Gloria," Jessamyn snapped, scrubbing harder, but I kept my eyes on Pa.

He had taken the bank man outside so we didn't have to hear him beg. But even with all Jessamyn's sloshing and scrubbing and scolding, I could still hear him say words like "loan," "please," and "one more week."

He could've said all that in front of me. Our things had been packed for weeks. Ma had already sent her wedding linen to Aunt May in Tulsa for safekeeping. I'd seen the look on the grocer's face when we came in. I'd heard Pa cursing at the fields and the sky and the rain, wherever it was. And I'd heard Ma and Pa whispering long into the night when we all should've been sleeping.

I knew what it meant when you didn't pay and didn't pay and didn't pay. I felt it in the worn-out knees of my overalls and in the empty part of my stomach. I could see it in the way Pa carried himself and in the way Ma looked out the window.

It wasn't our fault.

First the rain stopped falling. Then the wheat stopped growing. Then the dust storms started coming. Then the tractor stopped working, and the jars in the cellar started dwindling, and Pa stopped joking and joshing like the words dried right up in his mouth.

And then Ma got big. And Pa tried not to say *How we gonna feed one more kid* but we all knew he was thinking it. And Ma tried not to say *We've lost our minds bringing a baby into this world* but we all knew she was thinking it. I tried not to say how rip-roaring it would be to be someone's big sister, but they all knew I was thinking it. By the time Little

Si came screaming into the world, we all knew just to hold our tongues and stare that something so tiny and so perfect could come when there'd been nothing but bad news. He was scrawny and red as a cherry, but Ma was beaming because she said other than being fussy he was the healthiest baby she'd seen.

Maybe she was lying, but I don't think so. I just think when you're so small, you can't take as much dust into you as a girl like me can.

It was just me and Jess there in the kitchen, the two of us. It should've been three.

"Jess . . . ?" I mumbled into the washbasin.

"What."

I bit my lip. I was about to say something I knew I shouldn't. I'd been dancing around it all week since Pa had said quietly at supper that we were gonna have to leave our farm and head west for greener pastures and better work in California. I'd held my tongue when Jessamyn begged Ma not to kill the egg-laying chickens she had raised and given glamour names to. I'd held my tongue when Ma went out back and snapped Yvette and Rosalina's necks anyway. I'd held my tongue when Pa had taken apart the bed Jessamyn and I shared and sold it for scrap so he could get our pickup truck in shape for the drive. I'd held my tongue just like everyone else had held their tongue about whatever it was that was on their minds that was just too sad to say out loud.

Fat lot of good it'd done me. Or us.

"Don't you think the bank would let us keep the farm if they knew about Little Si?"

Jessamyn stopped scrubbing. She hadn't said a word about Little Si. Nobody had. Ma'd buttoned up her sorrow like a Sunday dress. And Pa kept his locked tight in his jaw.

"Well, don't you think?" I asked again.

Jessamyn was still behind me. Too still.

"He ain't even been in the ground two months. It ain't fair to kick us out."

Maybe we could get one more day, one more week. Maybe it would rain real good tomorrow or the day after, maybe the bank man didn't know, maybe if he knew he'd take his hat off and drive away and never come back.

"Jess?"

She didn't answer. So I kept on going.

"It ain't right. He's gotta say something. Pa's gotta say something. Maybe that bank man's got kids, too, maybe if he just knew what happened—"

CRACK!

The wet rag snapped across my bottom and I let a cussword fly.

"What did you say, Gloria?" Jessamyn snapped.

She yanked me back by the shoulder to give me her best big-sister stare. Water dripped off my hair and soaked into the straps of my overalls.

I mumbled what I said under my breath even though she knew darn well what I said.

"Speak up, Gloria."

"I *said*," I began loudly, "Jesus H. Ch—"

WHAP!

Jessamyn let that wet rag snap against my bottom one more time to make her point.

"Honestly, Gloria, why you gotta bring up stuff no one wants to talk about?"

Jess shoved my head back down so she could get in behind my ears. She was scrubbing and scrubbing like she could scrub away the bank man, the dust, and what lay buried beneath the old cottonwood. Like she could scrub away me knowing I'd heard her cry the night Little Si died. But I had heard her. And if she weren't so darned set about being contrary for the sake of it, I bet she'd be as mad as me about what was happening.

"So that's it?" I said. "You just gonna back down without a fight? You fine with leaving one of us here?"

Jess lowered her voice and hissed right into my ear, "You want Ma to hear you talking 'bout all this?"

My tongue went slack in my mouth. Truth was, I figured Ma might crack open like an egg if you didn't take enough care around her. Split right down the middle. Truth was, I could barely stand to be in the same room with her. We were silent for a good long while, Jess's hands hovering over me like they'd forgotten how to wash.

"Just keep out of it, Gloria," she said, almost soft enough to be a whisper.

"That's what you always say," I said.

"Well, that's what you always need to hear."

I waited for her to start in on me again, maybe even start yanking at the knots I knew were back there. But she didn't move. I peered over my shoulder and I could see her head held up high and alert. She was listening close to the sounds coming off the porch.

"It's almost done anyway," she said softly.

I gave a shove to the washbasin, sloshing some of the dirty water up and over the rim. There was a wet *splat* on the floor and Jess jumped back.

"Why you got to—Glo, you soaked my shoes!"

"Sorry."

"Why you got to make everything harder for everyone?"

"I ain't trying to—"

"You being a pill on purpose. You think 'cause

Ma and Pa ain't got time to mind you, you get to be a wild child?"

"I ain't a wild child, I just wanna stay!"

Jessamyn whipped me around and took my head in her hands like she was gonna knock some literal sense into me. She started to speak and then looked around to make sure no one was in earshot. "You think I *want* to go west? You think I *want* to leave my friends?"

"I think you wanna stay wherever Joe Franklin's sweet son is staying—"

Jess flicked her fingers against my ribs. Talking about Joe Franklin's boy always got to her.

"Honestly, Glo, is that all you can think about? I hardly got him on my mind. What I *got* on my mind is leaving this place and being stuck with no one to talk to but you. Minding you. Watching you. You like a stone around my neck."

"I ain't so bad—"

"Glo, you're the last person I wanna be in the back of a truck with for a thousand miles, or however long we driving for. Talking about your stupid baseball stuff, and—"

"It ain't stupid!"

"You thinking you're good enough to pitch for the Balko boys *is stupid*, Gloria. And I don't want to be hearing about it all the way to California."

It stung. Bringing up the Balko boys and the team they never let me play on.

"Well, I *am* good enough, they just ain't seen it yet—"

"No group of boys is ever gonna let a girl play ball with them."

"Well, why not?"

"I dunno, Gloria, that's just *how it is!*"

"Well, I could show 'em—"

"No you can't. Not hanging round them every day like a gosh-darn puppy dog."

She had a point. I'd been sneaking off whenever they practiced and hanging around the baseball diamond, waiting and hoping they'd give me a chance. For a moment that open field flashed through my mind, along with the sound of the bat hitting the ball into the sky. I could hear them all whooping for each other, getting louder each time a runner passed a base.

And then my eyes darted back to the porch window where Pa was raking his fingers across his cheek. Thinking about pitching suddenly *did* feel stupid.

"Fine, Jess, to heck with the Balko boys. But why ain't Pa fighting for us?"

Jess threw her arms up. "Pa ain't fighting 'cause there's no reason for us to stay. This place is dead, you hear? The land's dead. The tractor's dead.

The wheat's dead. The *sky* is dead, my chickens are dead . . . and . . . and *you know what else.*"

She whipped me back around to face her and dried her hands off on her skirt.

"Can you dry yourself off, or you need me to do that, too?"

"I ain't a baby."

"No?" Jess said, throwing me a dish towel. "Prove it."

I looked back over to Pa on the front porch talking to the bank man.

Just tell him about Little Si, I thought, *tell him what we been through, tell him what it was like, tell him we need a little more time.*

But instead I heard Pa say, "No, sir, I understand."

The words dropped down my insides like stones down a dried-up well. I felt them hit the bottom and turn to something ugly.

Sir. Pa had called him *sir.* Ma was tying the last of our stuff to the truck like she was getting paid to do it. Jessamyn clearly thought the best thing to do was to *give my hair a wash.* Things seemed to be about as upside down as they could be.

"Why I gotta be clean anyway?" I grumbled. "We just gonna get dirty on the road, you know Ma and Pa are gonna make me and you sit in the back."

Jessamyn rolled her eyes as far back in her head as they could go.

"You gotta be clean 'cause we gotta drive through town first. You gotta be clean 'cause you're Ma and Pa's little girl. You gotta be clean 'cause you're my little sister. If that's not enough for you, you gotta be clean 'cause given the circumstances, everyone's gonna think we oughtta *look like trash*. Don't prove 'em right, Glo."

I hardened all the muscles in my face. The ugly thing was putting down roots in my insides.

"Me looking like I'm fresh outta a shop window ain't gonna help us keep this farm and it ain't gonna bring Little Si back."

Jessamyn dropped her empty water bucket with a bang.

"Shut up! Honestly, Gloria, when will you learn that sometimes you gotta *shut up!*"

She snatched the washbasin, now filled with my dirt, rested it on her hip, grabbed the bucket, and stormed out back to toss the cloudy water. I wanted to tell her it didn't matter if she sloshed it out right here on the kitchen floor.

They were going to level our house anyway.

I watched Jessamyn's back as she disappeared through the screen door. Out back, Ma took a step towards her and asked her something. Jessamyn shook her head and threw up her free hand, gesturing towards me in the house. Ma put her hands on her hips and looked at the dirt.

They could talk about me all they wanted. Call me wild child and call me dirty. This was still our house. This was still our land. That was still my brother out back. And Pa hadn't signed any papers yet.

I put my hands on my own hips the way I saw Ma do it, but I didn't look at the ground. I stared straight out the front window at the bank man and caught the sun glinting off his silver watch chain. He looked out of place here, all polished up like he was. If he *knew*, if he *understood*, he wouldn't make us go. I knew it in my bones. I could walk right out there and stand next to my pa, take his hand and say—

Mr. Bank Man, let me set the record straight—

No, I'd say—

Mr. Bank Man, get off our land!

No, I'd say—

Mr. Bank Man, why don't you and I take a walk over to this cottonwood and I'll tell you some things you ought to know.

That sounded right. I cleared my throat and puffed up my chest to give me a little more courage than I had. This was what a hero would do in a picture, all lit up in silver. Step in and do what everyone said he shouldn't in the name of justice. No matter how they'd been wronged. Jessamyn would thank me later. They all would. I'd make the bank man feel sore about what he was up to, he'd give us another week, and the sky would prove Jessamyn wrong that it *wasn't* dead, and it would open up and soak the fields and little green shoots would come up like they used to and Pa would take my hands and say *Thank God for Gloria! We thought we were done for, but Gloria knew we had a chance!*

I started moving towards the front door. I walked through the dark hall, past the empty sitting room Ma had been so proud of. "I don't mind being a farmer's wife," she always said. "Long as I have a sitting room in my house."

Maybe if Ma could keep her sitting room she'd be less likely to break.

Maybe if a neighbor gave Jess two chicks she could rear them up and lay off giving me lip.

Maybe if Pa had his land he wouldn't be walking around so ashamed and talking so low, like he was embarrassed to be heard.

If no one was going to do anything, then I sure as heck was ready to step up.

I grabbed the front doorknob.

I turned it.

I stepped out onto the front porch, that bank

man's black hat eclipsing the sun, but he didn't scare me. Nothing could scare me now. Not after everything we'd been through. Out of the corner of my eye I saw Pa's red, raw eyes and the collar of his shirt fluttering in the breeze. It filled me up with all the words I needed to take back what was ours from the brink of losing it—

"Listen, here, mister," I said, "I got something to say—"

But all that breath for all those words burst right out of me as Ma's arms scooped me around the middle and yanked me back into the house, door slamming in my face.

Chapter Two

"Gloria, *don't you dare!*" Ma hissed, her palm pressing against my mouth.

I twisted around to see the bank man open a leather satchel full of bank papers. Papers that gave land and that took land. Papers that Pa was about to sign. I started twisting every which way I could and sent a howl straight into Ma's palm.

"*Gloria! Mae!*" Ma spat through her teeth.

Through the screen door, Pa took the pen, and I started kicking, but Ma was strong and she was clamping down around me like that big cottonwood growing roots as I wiggled and twisted and screamed into her hand.

I saw Pa take the set of papers and sign once, twice, three times. And I could feel Ma looking over my shoulder, watching it happen, too, not cracking, not crying.

And then it was done. I saw it in Pa's shoulders. I felt it in Ma's arms. And I heard a howling start in my ribs.

"Shh, Glo, shh," Ma whispered, cooing now like she would for a little baby, rocking back and forth like she could ease the storm out of me.

But the farm was gone.

And Ma had held me back. My lungs felt like they were made of fire. And something was heaving up in me that I had to get out. Something red and raw and violent.

"It's all right, Glo," Ma said. "You cry it out now. I got you."

Her words made me want to retch. I held still for just a moment for her to think I was done fighting, and her arms slackened just a little. With one thrust of my shoulder I broke free and scrambled out the back door, running away from Pa and the bank man's papers, bounding out into the blinding sun and over the dry, dead dirt.

Ma didn't even call after me.

I ran faster than I ever had before. Past our sorry windmill, past Jessamyn, who was probably wondering

why I was running and why Ma hadn't stopped me. I
ran before anyone could call me back, before anyone
could chase me down and tie me up and force me all
the way to California. I made it to the tree line and
stopped to catch the breath that was burning in my
chest. These were still my woods.

I hoped Ma realized what she'd done. I hoped
Ma was sorry. I hoped Ma was crying. I hoped Ma
would cry all the way to California. It was her fault
now. Her fault the house would get leveled. Her
fault we wouldn't be here to see the green shoots
of wheat come up when the world got right again.
Her fault Jess would never see Joe Franklin's sweet
son again. Her fault I'd never prove to the Balko
boys I was at least good enough to play outfield for
them.

Her fault I'd never get to sit under the cottonwood again.

I leapt down into the dried-out bottom of a creek
that used to sing with toads. I kicked the pebbles
along the sorry, hollowed-out space and listened
to them clattering like bones. I followed the creek
bed around to the edge of the wood where I could
see Pa talking to the bank man. Pa was far off, but
I could feel his hurting coming off him even from a
distance. Hurting right there out on the porch for all
the world to see, like he was some kind of spectacle.

The man reached into his waistcoat and offered Pa a cigarette.

"Don't take it, Pa," I said under my breath.

Pa took a long drag and closed his eyes like he was sipping honey.

I ground my heel into the dry, crackling earth. Pa had given up smokes months ago. He and Ma had been taking their coffee thin and black. I hadn't had milk since I couldn't remember when. We were all a little bit hungry and we were all a little bit hurting, but why'd he have to show it like that? Why'd he have to give the bank man the satisfaction of thinking he'd done him some kind of favor? He should've knocked the cigarette out of his hand, or at least blown smoke right under the brim of his fine black hat.

Everything was gone. The room we had all been born in, the room *Little Si* had been born in was going to get carted away in a heap of wooden planks and dusty plaster. No way was anyone going to try and make a home out of that shabby old farmhouse once we were gone.

There should have been yelling and fighting. We should have been standing, me, Pa, Jess, and Ma, with our arms linked on the porch daring them to take it all out from under us. Looking that bank man in the eye instead of staring at the ground like it was us who had something to be ashamed of.

I knew what would happen next. Pa would take that bank man's hand and shake it like some kind of fair deal had happened. Ma would climb into the front seat of the truck without saying a word and Jess would follow her. They'd call for me once and I'd come sulking out of the woods like a soggy cat. And then we'd drive off and say nothing about all the things we should have done and said.

But then I noticed the bank man's car.

It was long and silver and shiny with a big old hood ornament glinting on its nose. It was shining so bright I got to figuring that man had it wiped down and waxed right before he showed up on our doorstep just to make us feel small. Probably tossed a farmhand a nickel to do it. A man who would have had to say "Yessir," "Thankyousir," and "Rightawaysir."

Ma, Pa, and Jess could go down without a fight.

Not me.

Not this time.

I ran back into the creek bed to find the biggest rock I could throw. I pried it out of the dried-up dirt and ran to the edge of the woods.

And as my pa held that man's cigarette trembling between his teeth and as the man in black looked on to the house his bank was going to turn into a pile of timber, I walked out as far as I dared, hefted that stone up, wound it back behind me, said a prayer, and sent it flying.

The crack rang out like angels singing when that stone hit the windshield.

If those Balko boys could've seen that!

I dropped behind the trees.

The man in the suit swore.

Ma came running.

And then Jessamyn.

They were all talking over each other now, and I lifted my head to look through the branches and saw the man in the suit flapping his arms and pointing to a glorious crack running straight down his fine, waxy little windshield.

"This one of you?" he yelled. "This one of your stinking brood, Silas?"

"No sir," Pa said.

Pa was lying for me and I was grinning. He knew I had a good arm. He knew I'd been practicing all winter. Pa knew I'd cracked five birds outta the sky with it—we'd roasted the skinny things on sticks like hot dogs. "Could've knocked off Mrs. Homewood's Sunday hat without messing with a curl," Pa had said, smiling.

Pa wasn't smiling now, probably because that would let the bank man know the rock *was* from one of his stinking brood!

"You got some son I don't know about? Some scrawny little brat who thinks they're gonna bust up my car?"

Pa was standing tall.

"I got no sons," he said, his voice drifting off. "I got no sons . . . we only got girls here. It's me, my wife, and the girls."

Jessamyn nodded and Ma just stared ahead, her lips as thin as the cracks in the earth.

But I was smiling ear to ear, teeth and all.

The bank man said some words that I'd never heard anyone say out loud before. He ended with, "Just get. Get off the land. Take your trash and get."

I wasn't sure if "trash" meant Pa's stuff or Pa's family.

Pa nodded, took one more long drag of the cigarette, and stamped the butt out with his heel.

"Now," said the man in the suit. "I wanna see you go."

"Yes, sir," said Pa, and he nodded to Ma and Jess to get in the truck.

I watched as Ma walked as tall and calm as she could, holding one hand in the other. Pa helped Ma up into the front seat. He picked Jessamyn up and swung her into the back of the truck. She nestled in between the tightly rolled mattresses and piles of this and that. If the bank man had been thinking clearly, he would've noticed there was a spot cleared out for me.

Pa started up the truck and began driving off. The man in the suit was still scanning the trees looking for the boy who cracked his windshield. But he wasn't about to find me, or any boy for that matter. I started running. Running to where the road would bend and Pa and Ma would see me on their way into town. Running to where they'd scoop me up and give me kisses and say, *Boy, you showed that bank man what we Willards are made of!*

I ran through those woods, my house disappearing behind me. *My house.* The buckled-up wallpaper, the crack in the ceiling, the room where I was born, the corner of the porch where me and my friend Ella would tell secrets, the chicken coop where Yvette and Rosalina had laid us so many breakfasts, the shed where Pa kept his tools, the shanty and the outhouse with the spiders that sent Jessamyn screaming out as she pulled up her pants, the basket of Ma's mending work, the cellar with its jars of beans, the little baby quilt for Si we all sewed our initials into, Si's cradle, Si's cottonwood—

I could hear that truck rumbling.

"I'm coming!" I shouted. "I'm coming! Don't leave without me!"

I burst out to the road just as our truck came

slowly around the bend, teetering with the weight of everything we had, plus our hopes and prayers. Pa pulled up right beside me and slammed on the brake, sending a clatter up from the back.

"Get in, Gloria," Pa ordered. He wasn't smiling. He didn't say it with a wink. He said it like he was avoiding saying something else.

"Pa, I—"

"I swear to God, Gloria—"

Pa was spitting the words out like they tasted bad in his mouth. "I swear, Gloria, what on earth were you *thinking*?"

My throat was going dry again.

"I didn't mean to make you mad, Pa, I just thought—"

"Hush up. Don't you say a word. Just hush up and *listen*. You think I got a bank full of cash to pay for some man's car that my *daughter* busted up?"

"No, Pa, course not—"

"*I said hush up, Gloria!* In case it passed you by, we don't got much. What we got is in this car. That's it. There's nothing left. *Nothing*. Do you hear me? *We got nothing*—"

"Silas," Ma said, shaking her head, the same still expression on her face. "Save it. We gotta get on the road."

Pa's face was clouded over. He wasn't even looking

at me. But he held out his hand from the window, and I took it, pulling myself up and over to settle next to Jessamyn. The sun was high but I had goose bumps and my teeth started to chatter, or maybe it was my lip starting to tremble.

I knew better than to say anything else, even though words were swirling in my brain and pushing against my chest.

I looked into the front seat and saw the back of Ma's head. She had her fist in her mouth like it could stop any words from coming out. I watched as Pa put out a hand to rub the back of her neck. No one said anything on the way into town.

But as we turned the corner and the little collection of houses of Balko came into view, Jessamyn turned to me and lowered her voice.

"Don't tell Ma or Pa I said so, but I wished you'd smashed that car to pieces."

And for the first time I could remember, Jessamyn seemed like the only one who was rooting for me.

Chapter Three

Underneath me, I felt the truck rumble as we finally started to slow down.

Jess elbowed me in the ribs. "Look!"

I wiggled up and peered over the side. We'd been popping and groaning down the road for hours and hours. Up ahead was a huge camp of twinkling firelight and dozens of cars and trucks like ours pulled over by the side of the road.

No doubt Pa had spent all those miles dreaming up ways of making me pay for my sins. The sound of his voice barking at me to get in the back of the truck had been hammering in my brain since we'd left Balko for good. The more I thought about it, the more wrong it felt. Signing it all away without giving me a chance to fight for it. Screaming at me when I did fight for it.

All the way from Balko, I'd gripped the sides of the truck, staring hard out into the dead fields. I had let the wind dry my eyes and whip my hair against my cheeks. I'd cupped the air with my hand, dreaming I was slowing us down, just a little bit. Every time our truck hit a rock or a hole, I prayed a tire would just pop off. Just pop off and leave us within walking distance of our old farmhouse.

But it didn't. And mile after mile, Oklahoma slipped out from underneath us. Jess said something when we crossed the state line, but it wasn't for my ears. Maybe she was praying. Or saying goodbye to someone. But she sure wasn't talking to me.

As we slowed I could hear the bones of the truck popping and the engine just begging us to give her a rest already.

"Stopping here for the night!" Pa called from the front as he eased the truck to a stop by the side of the road. A rocky bluff rose up west of us, evening light sparking the top of it fire orange. The air was full of the sounds of men tinkering with their trucks. There was a *plink-plink* of hammers on metal that echoed against the bluff. It smelled like woodsmoke. And engine exhaust.

I knew what was coming next. A talking-to. A yelling-at. I stared hard at a box full of Ma's pans that read POWDERED MILK with a cow grinning too big on the side. Seeing that stupid cow with its stupid grin made me want to kick the darn thing over.

The driver's-side door opened and then slammed. Hard. And Pa's long shadow fell across my knees.

"You," he said. "Out. Now."

I pulled myself up and jumped down. The earth came up hard and fast, sending a shock through my legs. After hours of jostling, the world was fixed and firm again. I stood up tall, looking hard into the distance because I knew what Pa was going to do. He was going to try to make me feel ashamed of what I'd done. He was going to expect me to say I was sorry. To say I was wrong.

But I'd had just about enough of being told what to do and how to feel. I'd had just about enough of everyone thinking I wasn't worth talking to, or sharing plans with.

"Jess," Ma said. "Help me get supper started. Glo, you go with your pa."

Jess slipped out, quiet as a cat. I turned to look at Pa, right in the eyes.

His face was storming, a bead of sweat cutting a river right through the fine layer of dust at his temple.

His shirtsleeves were rolled up, the muscle cords in his arms tense and flexing. Around his cheeks, the beginnings of a rough-looking beard were starting to poke through.

"Let's move it," he said.

We started walking, not speaking and not looking at each other. Pebbles crunched underfoot with each step as we walked farther and farther from camp and towards that great rocky bluff. I figured the longer we walked on, the worse this whole thing was going to be.

"Stop," Pa said.

I stopped.

The camp was behind me and the sun was behind Pa. As he bent down to lean his palms on his jeans to look at me eye to eye, orange light blazed out from behind him.

"Gloria. Mae. Willard."

Every time Ma or Pa used my full name, I was in it real deep.

"I ain't never been as mad with one of my kids as I was today. *Never.* But I never raised a hand to you, and I'm not about to start."

A distant clatter of pots and pans sounded from the camp. I was breathing hard through my nose, words swirling inside me, ready to break loose and run wild.

"But Lord, Gloria, what were you *thinking*? I raised you better than that."

His voice was hard and sharp, but his words were what stung the most. My muscles went rigid to stop me from shaking, to stop me from being weak and soft.

"I raised you better than to be smashing things up and cussing at your sister and paying *no mind whatsoever* to your ma, so you just knock it right off, hear? I am damn tired, I am so damn tired, so you can just—"

"It isn't fair!" I shouted, and the bluff echoed it back right on cue.

Pa blinked. "Oh no?" he said, his face caught somewhere between astounded and furious.

"That's right!" I yelled. This was something new. Yelling at Pa. It felt wonderful and poisonous at the same time. "It ain't fair you just make us leave without telling us, without asking us—"

"Us?"

"*Me!* It ain't fair you just get to say when I stay, when I go. *Where* I go. You don't tell me nothing and then you screaming at me like I'm supposed to know better—"

"You *are* supposed to know better."

"You didn't ask me, you didn't even ask what I thought about leaving—"

"Because it *don't matter* what you think about leaving! It don't matter what any of us think about leaving, we just leaving because that's just the god-awful way it all fell out!"

"I wanna know things! Y'all treat me like the baby, I ain't the baby, you oughtta let me know what's going on—"

Pa threw back his head and laughed an awful laugh. "Oh, you wanna know what's going on? Tell me something, Gloria, you want to be part of things, huh? You want to walk into town every week for the last God knows how many months begging the bank to give you more time? Is that what you're missing out on? You want to ask the church board to feed your family because you can't? You want to ask the Homewoods, who ain't got much more than you, to pay for a stone for your *kid* 'cause you don't have the dough to do right by him yourself? Gloria, there are so many damn things I have had to ask for, hat in hand, you don't want to know. Believe me, you don't want any part of that."

It was like everything he'd kept pent up from the bank man exploded all over me.

I knew the ladies at church had been feeding us. I knew we owed at the grocer in town. And I knew about the Homewoods and the stone for Little Si. I was already living and breathing and dreaming about everything Pa thought he was keeping from me. And I knew it wasn't the knowing that was getting under my skin. It was the hearing it other places instead of from Pa's lips that made it bad.

I wanted to crumble into dust, blow away from this place and everything Pa was saying.

His breath was coming out shuffled up and broken and he kept opening his mouth like he could catch the words out of the air.

Finally, the fight went out of him and he got down on one knee and grabbed me by the shoulders.

"Gloria," he said, "after what we been through— no, after what your ma has been through—if that man had wanted to take me down to the sheriff's office and charge me with property damage or disorderly conduct, or who knows what, he could've. It's a miracle we're not down at the station right now, with you all selling every other thing we got to make bail."

I felt myself clamming up.

"Gloria, I'm gonna level with you. We are one step up from begging door to door. Where we're going, we'll be on someone else's land, in someone else's house. You can't run wild, you can't say the first thing that pops into your head, and you sure as hell can't go throwing rocks at whoever you happen to be mad at."

I nodded, wishing he would stop looking at me with his sore eyes.

"You can't—you just can't—you can't *be this way*, Gloria, I don't know how else to put it."

This way. I didn't know any other way to be.

"So just—just—" Pa shook his head and let his breath come out in a shake. "Just be *good* for me and your ma. Because we just can't—we just cannot take any more. Have I made myself clear, Gloria?"

I stared up at him. His face was less angry and more . . . just . . . *sad.* Back before things had gotten so bad, Pa used to crack jokes and play tricks on us, especially me because I fell for them every time. But ever since Little Si, he'd gotten all stony like that big bluff rising up—sharp, and rough, like he'd probably fall apart if you hit him in the right place. And suddenly I *was* sorry. Not for what I'd done. The bank man deserved to have his window busted and all his tires popped as far as I was concerned. I was sorry for the hurt that was painted across my pa's face, clear as day. Maybe it'd been there all along. But I hadn't seen it there before. Not like this.

Every part of me wanted to throw my arms around him, say I was sorry if it would make him feel better.

But I just stood up tall and said, "Yes, sir," as solemnly as I could.

We both stood looking at the ground for a while,

like real men do when they're being noble about not saying what's in their hearts. I felt a little wind at my back like the swell of violins in the pictures. I lifted my head up, squinting my eyes into the setting sun. Might as well try to make things right.

"I'm sorry I caused you to worry, Pa, and if you give me a chance, I'll do right by you."

He must've been surprised, because the darting went out of his eyes and there he was looking down at me, holding up his jaw like he was holding up the whole world.

"All right, Glo. I said what I needed to say to you. Go on, get back."

"Yessir," I said, and turned to go.

I could feel Pa standing and staring behind me as I walked. Probably making sure I was heading back to camp and not about to run off with a circus or something.

Maybe they'd take a wildcat like me.

"Hold up, Glo," Pa's voice called out behind me.

I stopped in my tracks and turned.

Pa was looking off into the sky, the way he used to do when he was looking for rain. He put his hands on his hips and raked the dirt with the tip of his boot.

"'Bout how far off would you say you were . . . when you threw that rock?"

The wind picked up a little.

"I was at the creek, Pa. Pulled a stone outta the creek bed."

Pa cocked his head my way.

"All right . . . what were you aiming for?"

This was a trick. The answer to this question would finally earn me a smack on the bum. No use lying. Best to get it over with.

"I was . . . aiming at his car, Pa. I was aiming to break a window."

Pa nearly jumped out of his boots. His arms flew up and then crossed again and he kept shaking his head and looking at the dirt and looking at the sky and then looking at me.

"Kid," he said. "You either got lucky, or you got the arm of a boy twice your size."

It was like the sun was painting my name across all the rocks.

"Now, you go on back to your ma and help with whatever she needs helping with. I gotta take a walk. Just gotta do some thinking. Go on now, before I change my mind about letting you off this easy."

"Yes, sir," I said again, and Pa walked off into the sunset and I headed back towards camp, singing some old campfire song about sleeping under the stars.

Chapter Four

Pa didn't show for dinner. I guessed he was probably working through his troubles on his own, or maybe bottling them up to explode later.

We ate without him.

The cinnamon-colored land had started to turn cold and blue. Little kids were running around now, glad to be out of their hot cars. A few cigarettes burned pink and floated in the dark. Somewhere, a deep laugh echoed off the bluff and disappeared up to the evening, where just a couple of piercing white stars were showing off. We'd be sleeping without a roof tonight with nothing but the oilcloth pitched out like a tent from the side of our truck, thin mattresses rolled out in the Texas dirt. I wondered how big the spiders were here. I wondered when we would have a place of our own again.

"Glo," Ma said, fussing with the oilcloth. "Go find your pa. I need his help to get us set."

She said it without looking at me, like everything that had happened back at the farm and between me and Pa just now was a million miles behind her. I didn't argue.

"Yes, ma'am," I said, and started off through the open air to find him.

I wound my way through the campsites scattered across the open land. Some folks I could hear fighting. Some folks I could hear singing. At one point someone's ma called out from a fire glow, "You lost, little girl?" I quickened my step.

"No, ma'am!" I called over my shoulder. "It's my pa who's lost, and I'm aiming to find him."

"Menfolk got a game going," she called out, and pointed. "Might find him there."

I went off the way she had pointed, hoping I'd find him soon. Wondering if I'd be able to trace my way back once the sun snuffed out. The land was wide and lonely, and it was getting darker by the minute. And there were strangers everywhere.

Just how many trucks of folks were ahead of us, or already in California? We'd pulled over by the side of the road for the night, but there had to be others that were going to drive till the morning and beat us there. Maybe there *was* no work. Maybe tonight was the first night of sleeping under an oilcloth for the rest of my life. The thought made the sky bigger, deeper. It made the air colder and the ground feel hollow under my feet. I'd seen folks be on their own with the cards stacked against them in the pictures. Cowboys and pirates and even regular Joes just down on their luck. I guessed I was just feeling now what they were feeling then. Like the whole world was waiting to see me stop hoping. Waiting to see me give up.

I tried whistling as I walked. It took the edge off my worry, but that was it. I walked until I crossed over the lip of a little hill that panned out flat beyond. And there was Pa.

He was sitting on the ground watching a game of baseball that had started up. He was staring straight ahead like he was at the church game that happened every Saturday in July. Last time that had happened had been when the grass was still green and the crickets were hopping. Here, everything was all long plateaus, rocks, and open night sky.

There was just a little bit of light left, and I was pretty sure the men would have to pack up any moment, even though the stars looked like they'd be something fierce and bright. I watched as the players shuffled back and forth on their bases or crouched down so they'd be ready to run. I listened to their voices bouncing off the rocks beyond and their whistles shooting up to the sky. I'd watched a million games before and practiced pitching till I thought my right arm would fall off. I'd never played in a single one. No one had ever asked me.

"Hey there, Pa," I said quietly when he didn't notice me standing beside him.

He turned his tired face towards me. Everything about him that had been hard and stony had gone soft around the edges.

"Hey, sweet Gloria," he said, and patted the earth beside him for me to sit.

Hadn't expected that. I couldn't remember the last time I'd been sweet at all. That was more Jessamyn than me. I reckoned I was a bit salty. Or sour. Or something. I sat down beside him all the same.

The ground had gone cold and my arm prickled up, all gooseflesh. As we sat together, a familiar ache crept back into my chest. It was the sort of tightness you feel when you're holding your breath at the bottom of a pond. And it had been there awhile between me and Pa, long before I threw that rock. But it was sharper now that we'd had words. Less like someone was standing on your chest and more like they were pulling piano wire across it. I wanted to ask him what he was thinking. I wanted to ask him why he thought I couldn't handle knowing things. I wanted to ask him why he hadn't fought for us and when he'd given up. And I wanted to ask him why he hadn't come to find me when he saw a baseball game was going.

But instead I said, "Who's winning?"

Pa let out a chuckle. "No one's winning," he said. "Not a single run."

Just like that, a batter struck out and his team threw their arms up and shook their heads.

I twisted around to look behind me. The campfire light burned warm below the cold white stars up in the blue.

"There's an awful lot of people here," I said.

"Yeah."

"They all going to California like us?"

"Yeah."

"Must be a lot of work out there."

"Mmm."

"What happens if we get out there and there's nothing left for us to do?"

Pa didn't say a thing, but his shoulders went brittle and stiff. He scanned the wide-open space and kept taking in breath to speak before stopping himself and flipping his hat over in his hands. I guessed it was just like that between us now. Stopping and starting and never getting anywhere. And then, after a long stretch of silence—

"Don't you worry about it. Just let me worry about it for you, huh, Gloria? Can you let me do that?"

There was nothing to do but nod.

In front of us, the final batter came up to a home base made out of the top of a coffee tin. He spat the way they're supposed to on a real team and swung a few practice rounds.

"Your granddad used to play with me," Pa said out of nowhere. "Taught me to throw, taught me to hit, taught me to run fast . . ."

He trailed off and looked up at the star-thickening sky.

"Guess I always thought I'd do the same with my son."

He let that last word hang there in the dark like he'd never seen me throwing stones up into the sky. Like he'd never heard me talking about the Balko boys. Like he didn't remember the time I asked him to show me how a game worked with four bottle caps for bases and a handful of dried beans for players.

I waited for him to remember. But he just stared

ahead. And then he suddenly took in a big breath of air like he was waking up after a long sleep.

"Never mind that, Gloria. You, your sister, and your ma are all I need."

I forced my lips into some sort of smile. The smile felt like the biggest lie I'd ever told. And I had fibbed a lot.

THWACK!

The batter finally made a hit. We rose to our feet as the ball sailed into the stars. The batter started running. He ran and ran, even though we knew that ball was gone, it was a home run for sure! His teammates cheered and cheered. Pa put his fingers into his mouth and let out an ear-piercing whistle that went right up to the rising moon.

He smiled at me.

"Ate your supper?"

I nodded. "Sure did. You get anything?"

"You let me worry about that."

I crossed my arms across my chest. "Ma needs your help getting the oilcloth set and all."

"Yup," he said, sliding his hands into his back pockets. "C'mon."

I held back.

"You go on, I'll be right behind you."

Pa narrowed his eyes at me.

"Not gonna dawdle, are you, Glo?"

"No, sir."

"Getting dark."

"I know it."

"Don't be five minutes behind me."

"Yessir."

And Pa walked off, leaving me in the wide-open space, a ribbon of pale blue licking at the horizon.

Part of me wanted to stay out here all night, listening to the sky and the wind whispers, letting my thoughts settle under the moon. Ma always said being under a night sky gave her the same feeling as being in a church. She said sometimes it was easier to feel God listening when it was just you and the heavens.

I wasn't sure I'd ever been certain that God was listening. Even if he was listening right now, I wasn't sure what to say or ask for. All I could think of was what I *didn't* want. I didn't want to be kept out of things. I didn't want Jess to think I was a stone around her neck. I didn't want Ma and Pa to keep me in the dark about everything. I didn't want to be the kind of person people think is a waste of time.

I wanted to belong somewhere, even if it wasn't Oklahoma. I wanted to be someone people listened to, even if I was loud sometimes and maybe said the wrong thing once in a while. I wanted to be someone you could tell your secrets to, and look up to, even if I wasn't going to be a big sister. And I wanted to play ball for real, not just by myself, knocking old apples out of a tree with a creek stone, or watching everyone else play. I wanted to be on a team.

"You listening?" I said out loud.

Stillness, darkness, and quiet.

Just me and the moon.

It had inched up higher into the sky. It was as round as one of Mrs. Homewood's nice china plates and it made everything shimmer a little silver. It was the kind of thing you might miss if you were sitting in a hot kitchen around a table and not out under the open sky. It was icy white, sharp and clean in the blackening blue.

But then I saw it wasn't the only moon out there.

There was a shadow moon gleaming below, a pale, soft blue against the dark. I stood up and squinted into the night. The shadow moon was perfect and round, glowing as dim as a faraway firefly.

It was the baseball, sitting in the dark, watching me.

The air grew sweet and chill. I blinked a couple times to make sure I wasn't imagining it. But it just seemed to glow brighter each time my eyes snapped open.

I could feel its weight in my hand. I already knew it would fit in my large overall pocket. I knew its red stitching might as well spell out my name.

"No more brooding," I said out loud. "No more waiting, no more begging."

I was going to pluck that ball out of the dust, brush her off, and keep her close.

No matter what else happened, the next time I found a game going, I wasn't going to be sitting on the sidelines.

Chapter Five

THUDsssss.

The ball hit the red Arizona rock, sending a cloud of rusty smoke up around it.

Jess slapped the sides of her skirt and gave a little huff. Ma had sent her off to keep me occupied and out of her hair. Normally when Ma wanted me out of the kitchen, Jess would walk me into Balko to the little picture house on the main drag. The manager's son was sweet on her, and he'd wave us on in, sometimes even pour us a soda pop. But there was no picture house out here by the side of the road to sneak into. Just wide-open space, me, and my baseball.

Jess was less than thrilled at having to mind me,

let alone having to play ball with me. But Ma said so and that was that.

"All right, then," Jess said, "you got me. Strike."

She bent down and shook the baseball out of a sandy pit. Jess was swinging a dead old branch for a bat and she was none too happy about it. Behind her, a big rock stuck up outta the earth like God was trying to hitch a ride to California, too. With each miss the ball hit the side of the rock, or skidded into the rusty earth. And each time Jess slapped the dust off her skirt, shook the red dirt off the baseball, and flung it back to me.

"I ain't even got a real bat," she grumbled, and gave the ball a halfhearted toss.

Jess was a rotten thrower, but I didn't mind. I never knew which way the ball was going to go; scuttering along the dirt, sailing high above, or speeding right towards my nose. Anyone else might have been annoyed. But I figured when I played on a team, I had to be quick and ready to pounce. Jess didn't know it, but she was the best person I could've practiced with.

THAP!

The ball slapped the inside of my palm. It weighed the same as a good throwing stone but was round and perfect and warm in the sun. It had been smooth and cool a few nights ago, nestled between the Texas rocks. I'd sure gotten a talking-to when I'd come back to camp after promising Pa I'd only be five minutes behind him. But I was glad I found it. I would have been thinking about it all the way to California if I'd left it sitting lonely in the dark.

Jess blew all the air out of her lips and let her head sink down the way you do when you don't wanna be exactly where you are. It was strange seeing my sister, who cut up starlet pictures and placed them carefully inside a coffee tin out here, with a stick bat playing at baseball.

"All right, Glo, how long you gonna be throwing at me for?" she said, standing up straight and leaning her hand against the blackened branch.

"I gotta practice! Ain't nobody gonna have a reason to pass me up when we get to California!"

A car rumbled past on the road, kicking up dirt and clattering like a box of teakettles.

Jess cocked her hips.

She was getting tired of this and stood with the tip of the branch buried in the dirt.

"C'mon, now!" I called. "You're gonna miss if you're not ready!"

Jess twisted the branch into the dirt, making war with some root, or something. "I been missing this whole time, Glo."

"That's just 'cause you ain't had practice! C'mon,

I'll throw you an easy one! I can throw it slow, Jess, I can!"

I was standing a good ways away, but I could swear I saw her face go a little scarlet. Her lips moved, but I couldn't make out what she was saying.

"What? Whaddya say?"

Her whole body flexed.

"I said, just throw the darn ball and get on with it!"

"Whatever you say, ma'am!"

I pulled it back, my left leg coming up with it, and let her fly.

THUDsssss.

Jess jumped back from the dirt cloud like she was getting tired of its nonsense.

"All right, I didn't say hurl it at me like you was trying to kill that rock, just go normal!"

The heat coming off the earth was shimmering in the distance like an oil slick.

"That *was* normal!" I called out. "You just getting slow! I'm just warming up!"

Jess's hands went to her hips and she pitched forward a little.

"Look, Glo, if you're gonna be a pill, you can go find someone else to throw at, I got stuff to do!"

"Oh yeah?" I called. "Like what? It ain't like you can run off and make moony eyes at Joe Franklin's sweet son like you do after church!"

It was like I'd thrown water on a cat.

"What do you know about—Glo, I ain't done no moony eyes at no boy *never*! 'Specially not the kind that's whistling and smiling like a fool all the darn time—"

"Yeah, he got a real nice smile, Jess!"

"I swear, Gloria Mae, you got the biggest mouth on you—What do you know? Who you been talking to? I ain't done *no* moony eyes and you know it!"

I grinned. I had her like a June bug on a string.

"I swear, Gloria," she went on, "if I find out you been following me around—"

"Aw, so you *was* making moony eyes!"

"I didn't *say* that, Glo—"

"Aw, heck, Jess, just throw the darn ball back to me!"

"*Listen*," she said, reaching for the ball, "when we get where we're gonna get to, you gotta find your own kind. I don't want no scrappy kid sister spying on me—"

She shook the dust off the ball—

"—when I got to be having my own life, with folks that ain't running around like my shadow and—"

"*Throw the ball, Jess!*"

"—folks that ain't running around like my shadow, sneaking behind—"

"*Jess,* it ain't *nothing* to be sweet on Joe Franklin's son, everybody knows he's sweet on you!"

"*First off,* Gloria Mae, Joe Franklin's son's name is *Benjamin*, which ought to be easy to remember."

Something jostled in my brain about a kite and a lightning storm.

The heat was rising up from the earth but I could swear it was coming off Jess's face hotter than our tired engine. She stood stock-still for a minute, her lips curling inwards like she was afraid of blabbing something I didn't know, and then her nose twitched like a hare's and—

Shoop! SLAP!

She threw that ball straight as an arrow, flaming hot, right into my palm.

I dropped it and shook my arm, little lightning bolts of pain flashing from shoulder to fingertip.

Jess hitched the branch up over her right shoulder, her eyes sharp.

"Throw the ball."

I did.

She swung and missed, but this time was different. Her swing was hard.

"Catch," she commanded, throwing it back to me.

I did. She sent it straight and true.

Again, she hoisted the bat over her shoulder and bent her knees, rocking back and forth a little.

"*Second*, Gloria Mae Willard, if you had half a brain, you'd notice that *Ben* flashes his smile at every girl in Balko. 'Cause he's got no decency. 'Cause he's gotta make every girl fawn and fool over him. 'Cause he *likes* being liked. 'Cause maybe he saw his daddy do it or maybe his momma never told him it *ain't right to lead girls on*—and I *swear to God*, Gloria, throw the ball!"

I did.

THUDsss.

Jess went for it like a pointer dog and hurled it back to me.

I was ready for her throws now, sharp and slicing through the air. I was catching them just right, making sure my arm was firm but loose so the shock of it wouldn't race down my arms into my shoulders.

Jess swung the branch up once more, looking me in the eye all the while. I drew up the ball, feeling every cord of muscle tense and flex.

"Thirdly, *Gloria*, I don't have time for boys like that—*I don't have time for boys*, they got heads full of nonsense and they don't know how to talk nice, and they don't know how to dress nice, and they certainly don't smell nice, not any boy and especially *not Joe Franklin's son whose name is Benjamin Lawrence Franklin which you should know 'cause he sits behind us in church every Sunday!* Now *throw!*"

There was a shattering of dried wood as the branch exploded in Jess's hands.

She'd hit it.

And either I threw so hard or she swung so good that the wood couldn't take it and broke into splinters.

Maybe it was both.

"Gol-lee, Jess, you got it!"

Jess looked into her hands at the stub of wood she still clutched, astonished. And then she caught herself looking wide-eyed and shook it off, sending a brilliant gaze my way that beamed and spun through the air like spider silk.

"Course I did," she said. "Now go find me a better branch."

Walking back to our truck, Jess swung her branch with each step. The world was getting quiet and cold and blue, but I could still feel the sun's heat baked into my skin and I knew it would keep me warm for a while. I'd shoved the ball into the large pocket of my overalls, same as I used to do with apples when our tree was still bearing fruit. Somehow, this was sweeter.

Jess's heat had vanished with the setting sun and she was calm and cool like she was heading to Sunday school. Her skirt kicked about her knees and the evening light painted her cheeks and collarbone a milky sort of silver. We walked shoulder to shoulder, or I guess, my head to her shoulder since she'd shot up like a new sapling and I didn't show any sign of catching up. I couldn't remember the last time my sister wasn't walking five steps ahead of me or shrinking back telling me to go on!

"Jess?" I piped up, my voice tiny in the big open desert.

"Mmm-hmm?" Jess replied without looking at me.

I could see a cooking fire flickering from our camp.

"Joe Franklin's son does smile at all the girls. I seen that, too."

She said nothing, but the first night bug started trilling.

"But I also know that he hasn't always sat behind us in church. He started sitting there after Miss Claire told the whole class 'bout what a whiz you were with words."

Ahead, the outline of Ma was waving a dish towel at us.

"And sure, he does look at all the girls. But he looks at you different. And I know 'cause I seen him looking at you when you weren't looking at him . . ."

Jess's long even steps slowed.

"And he wasn't smiling at all. Just looked . . . kind of . . . peaceful, I guess."

Pa was standing next to Ma now.

"Besides," I went on, "if the Franklins did pack up and go to California, I can't see how you won't see him again."

Even though I was afraid to look at her because I didn't want a talking-to and I'd already said more than I should've, I could feel her smile coming off her like the cheers of a faraway crowd.

Part Two

Chapter Six

"Would you look at that . . . ," Jess murmured, hanging out over the side of our truck.

Up ahead was the biggest orchard I'd ever seen. It was green and lush and full of ripening fruit. "Peaches," Pa had said the night before, "we're gonna go pick peaches."

Of course, he'd said we were going to pick a lot of things. Trouble was, folks like us were a dime a dozen, all showing up at the same places for the same lousy buck. California had been nothing but looking for work, waiting for work, and watching our potatoes go down, spud by spud.

Being hungry wasn't half so bad as having a right

arm that was about as good as a wet rag. Couldn't remember the last time I'd asked Jess to let me practice with her. Best I could do was pull my baseball out of my pocket and roll it around in my hand. We were just so plumb tired at the end of each day, and the moment my head hit the mattress I was dreaming of roast beef sandwiches and bacon sitting on a mountain of eggs. Looking out at all that blushing rosy fruit made my tongue go sweet. My mind didn't even need to turn it into pie, or jam, or cobbler. Just one bite of one peach straight off the tree would be enough to send me running again and leaping into the sky.

Pa pulled our popping, moaning truck up to a great white gate. And standing in front of that gate was a man in pressed white trousers and a wide-brimmed hat. He looked about as friendly as St. Peter to a bunch of sinners. Like we ought to be just a little bit ashamed to be asking for work. Behind him was a man holding a clipboard, twisting a toothpick between his lips and staring us down like he was getting paid to do it. He probably was.

The man in the white hat looked our truck up and down and stepped forward, sun glinting off his belt buckle. The man with the toothpick held back and just watched. I felt jittery and about to explode. I looked over at Jess and I could see she had her fingers crossed on both hands.

St. Peter in his white hat stepped up to Pa's window.

"Name?" he said, flat and bored-like.

"Willard," answered Pa.

"How long you been in California?"

"One month."

"You up to hard work?"

"Yes, sir."

"Well, we got plenty. You either work in the trees, in the sorting house, or in the cannery."

"Sounds just fine."

"How many you got?"

"Two grown and able-bodied, two young and able-bodied."

The man with the toothpick was writing everything down on his paper and taking his sweet time to do it. Every time he finished writing down one of our answers, he flipped the toothpick over once and nodded to the man in the white hat to keep going. *C'mon!* I thought. *Get me in that peach orchard, I'll be up a tree so fast you'll think my granddaddy was a cat!*

"Long as you're bringing in your share I don't care how many you got," said the man in the white hat. "Rent's the same whether you got two pickers living in there or twenty."

Pa cleared his throat.

"If it's all the same to you, we'll sleep in our tent."

I shut my eyes and saw spots. I didn't want to sleep in a tent. It wasn't a tent. It was an oilcloth pitched out from a truck covered in dirt and smelling like gasoline.

The other man looked up, balanced his toothpick to the side, and stopped writing.

"It's not all the same to me," said St. Peter. "You all may not care about sanitation back where you come from, but we expect every man, woman, and child to meet hygienic standards. You work here, you live here. And you pay rent. Don't like it, I got enough folks I can find that don't ask questions about why we do things here the way we do them. Understand? Or do I need to repeat myself a little slower?"

My jitters had developed a sort of edge. And I needed to pee, so I sat on my foot.

"Why's this taking so long?" I whispered to Jess.

"Shut up," she whispered back.

Pa looked like he was about to argue with the man, and Ma cut in.

"We can rent. We'll be working, we're happy to pay rent."

If I hadn't been sweating so bad and clenching my jaw, I would've cheered her on.

"Rent's six dollars a week."

I turned to Jess and whispered, "Boy, they must pay real good here and have some nice house with that kind of dough!"

"Gloria, *shut up!*"

The man with the toothpick cleared his throat. "And with electricity it'll be eight, come Saturday."

"Eight!" Pa said.

Ma's voice was extra cool and collected. "Sir, we're right tired at the end of the day. We'll do just fine without."

St. Peter put his hands on his hips and the man with the toothpick chuckled up at the sun.

"See, there you go doing it again. Asking questions, making demands. Houses come with electricity. You don't want it? You can drive on up the road and ask at Michelson's Apricot Grove what they got going, but I hear they've got all the hands they need there, not to mention they take all kinds of folks. Peaches are almost through, so you can take a couple weeks of guaranteed work and pay for electricity while you're at it, or you can try your luck elsewhere. Say, Willard, you let your wife do an awful lot of the talking."

Ma and Pa were silent. The edges in my jitters were starting to slice me up a little inside, and my bladder was making it hard to think straight.

"All right now," St. Peter went on. "We only

need just a few more folks for the picking season. The way it works here, we front you rent and electric for your first week, you pay up on Saturday. Quit before then, I'll have you arrested for theft. Done it before. We got a store on-site, and you can get most of what you need right there, no need to be going into town. Since you folks look like you ain't got much to buy with, you'll buy on credit. You pay up at the end of the week with your rent and electric. Sounds good?"

"Sounds good," Pa said quietly.

"Good. Picking's about done for the day, folks'll be coming in soon. You start tomorrow, but your rent starts tonight. Couple more rules. No stealing the product. That's an easy one. You want something to eat, go to the store. This isn't a government camp here, we don't do handouts. And no drunkenness, no gambling. Those are grounds for expulsion. And no organizing. Whatsoever. You got that?"

"I got that," said Pa.

"'Cause we had trouble here a few days ago and we won't stand for that."

Pa nodded.

I wondered why on earth the man in the white hat was so bent on us not organizing peaches.

St. Peter looked over to the man with the toothpick and nodded. I was squirming fierce and wobbling back and forth on my foot. Then he walked around to the back to take our license number. I felt Jess fidget next to me and saw that the man with the toothpick was looking right at her. He smiled a little and made the softest kissy noise I'd ever heard. The boys at school did the same thing at whatever girl was taller than them, but they were always loud, laughing. This was quiet, like Jess was the only one supposed to hear it. I poked her in the side, but she just swatted my hand away.

"You girls stand up," St. Peter said.

Jess stood and I crouched down low, thinking I might just explode if I had to move. But Jess took my hand and slowly pulled me up. I twisted my legs together as tightly as I could while she folded her arms across her chest.

"You girls got lice?" the man asked.

"No, sir," said Jess.

"You got worms?"

"No, sir."

"You keep yourself clean?"

"Yes, sir."

My breath was coming in little shudders, and I was swaying side to side.

"Something wrong there? Cat got your tongue?"

Oh Lord. Oh Lord I had to pee. "Mmm-mmm, no sir."

"Why you fidgeting, girl, you got fleas?"

"Mmmmm no, sir, I just . . ."

I had to. I had to tell him. I needed to go. "It's just, sorry, sir, can I—I mean, *may* I—Do you, you got a—Sir, I gotta take a leak real bad."

I heard Jess let out her breath.

"Oh, Gloria." Her voice sounded like disappointment. Or embarrassment.

The man in the white hat let out a laugh and I could hear the fella behind him snickering. "Yeah, we got toilets. Just west of the houses."

My face was hot and my blood was pumping like electric wire.

"Thanks, sir, honestly, thank you."

The man slapped the back of the truck.

"Number seventy-two. That's your place. For now."

He nodded and the gate opened up. I could feel his eyes laughing at me, and I hated him for it. He stood with his arms across his chest, smiling as we went by. I turned to Jess and said, "What's wrong with organizing peaches anyway?" The man must have heard me because he turned around and said just loud enough for me to hear, "Them Okie kids are about as dumb as they are dirty."

He was laughing, and I felt like he'd slapped me across the face.

Chapter Seven

I busted out of the outhouses with my hand over my nose from the stink, but at least I could think straight again. Sanitation and hygiene, my eye! I pumped some water at the sinks and scrubbed my face and neck with it. Far as I knew I wasn't dumb. But I was dirty. That much was true. Pa was back at the truck in front of number 72, which I'd barely got a look at as I was running to the toilets. Ma and Jess had gone to the company store to scrounge up something to eat. I shook the water from my face and got my first good look at the camp.

My heart fell a little. The man had said *houses*. I'd lived in a house. Might've needed some work, might've needed some paint, but I'd had a *house*. These were something else. Like little stick shacks all stuck together in rows that went on for days. *Houses* were supposed to have second floors. These were short and squat. *Houses* were supposed to have rooms. From the looks of it, these were one-room cabins. And all around us were fences. Fences and fences and more fences. Fences around the peaches and fences around the shanties. Like they didn't want us to get out. And they sure as heck didn't want us climbing over to pick ourselves a peach. Must've thought we were all thieves. Funny, people thinking I was like to steal made the whole idea just a little bit more attractive.

"Hey, you," said a voice.

I turned to see a boy about my age staring me down with a blade of grass twisting in his mouth. He took a slow step down from his own one-room stick shack. His shirt was stained and yellow, his jeans were soft and sun-bleached. His eyes had a steely gleam to them that promised a tussle and a shiner if crossed.

"Hey yourself," I said.

The side of his mouth twitched like he wanted to grin. I'd been around long enough to know he was sizing me up, and like a tomcat, I felt my hair go spiky and my limbs get ready to pounce.

He took the blade of grass between his fingers

like a cigarette and spat something black into the dirt.

"You new here."

It wasn't a question, so I didn't answer.

"You in seventy-two?"

I nodded.

So did he.

"So you the one taking Jimmy's place."

"Who's Jimmy?"

The boy just stared me down, twisting the blade of grass over and over between his fingers. A branch snapped underfoot behind me and I spun around to see another boy standing there, thin as a sapling with a mess of brown-black hair.

"I saw you come in on that old truck," said the sapling boy in a voice that sounded about as clear and sunny as a church bell. "Where from?"

"Oklahoma," I said.

The sapling boy's face lit up like the Fourth of July.

"I knew it," he said. "Whereabouts? Turpin? Arnett? Floris? I've got cousins all over, east to west, north to south."

His voice had a twang like mine but was made of finer stuff. Like his pa was a preacher and his ma taught Sunday school.

"Balko," I said. "I'm from Balko."

The sapling kid put his fingers to his lips like it could help him think.

"Balko, Balko, Balko . . . ," he murmured, and then his bright eyes flashed back to mine. "I've heard that name before . . . not sure *where*, it'll come to me. My name's Quentin. How long you been on the road?"

I started to answer, but I'd just barely opened my mouth when I heard another kind of sound behind me.

Thap.

It was the sound of leather slapping palm. The sound a baseball makes when you pop it high in the air and catch it bare-handed. It made my arm itch and the world come into sharp focus. I turned back to the boy with the blade of grass. He was holding a baseball in his right palm, like he'd plucked it out of the air. His eyes were fixed on me, but still as he was, I gathered he could run, pounce, or duck in the blink of an eye if he had to.

"This the new kid taking Jimmy's place?" came another voice. And there was a third boy, this one tall as the day was long, with one of those thick necks that told me he'd either been baling hay his whole life or throwing punches. Probably both. His shoulders seemed broader even than Pa's, and he must have shot up recently because his pants didn't even come close to covering his ankles.

But that wasn't all.

In his right hand, he was swinging a baseball bat. There was a whisper of a hiss each time it kissed the ground. He came right up behind the boy with the baseball and now there were six eyes on me. Watching and waiting.

This was getting interesting.

Three boys, one baseball, one bat, and a missing kid called Jimmy. As dirty and dust-covered as this shantytown was, I was starting to think there might be more for me to do here than pick peaches. All you needed was a handful of players to make a team. I felt a humming through my ribs and a hunger in my belly. Back in Balko I might have started begging for a chance to play. But not here, not now. I had a thousand miles at my back, ten thousand pitches under my arm, and I'd seen enough pictures to know how to put a little swagger in my step. I hooked my thumbs in the sides of my overalls and squinted up at the sky.

"So y'all play ball here or are thems just for show?" I asked, cocking my head at the bat.

The baseball kid grinned. "I'd say we legitimate."

The other two boys quickly nodded. It was getting real clear that the kid with the ball was the boss of this operation.

"So then," I said slowly, wishing I had spent as much time learning to spit out the side of my mouth as I had learning to throw, "where y'all play round here? Guessing the bosses don't take kindly to batting in the orchard."

The boss kid was still as a picture, his grin frozen.

"Aw, you know, we got a place," said the tall kid with the bat. "We play right around—"

"*Ahem,*" said the boss kid. The tall kid blinked and shoved his free hand in his pocket.

"What he means," the boy called Quentin said carefully, "is that the *locale* is what you'd say *top secret.*"

The familiar weight of disappointment pulled at my arms. That was the kind of thing boys said to keep you out. The kind of thing I might have listened to before and just gone home. This time, I forced a shrug like it didn't mean a thing and stayed put.

"Fair 'nuff," I said. "Well, *when* you play anyway?"

"How we know you ain't a spy?" asked the tall kid with the bat.

"A spy?" I asked. Maybe it was a California thing, but I'd never heard of a baseball spy before.

Boss kid tossed it from one hand to the next. "You ain't been here long, but you best know the bosses got eyes and ears crawling all over this place looking for *radical activity*."

I didn't know what radical activity was. So I acted like I did.

"I don't see what *radical activity* got to do with baseball," I said.

The boys looked to one another.

"Well, in any case, you can't be too careful these days," I said.

I looked off in the distance like I wasn't hanging on their every move. That was when I saw two more boys looking on. Maybe they'd just gotten there, maybe they'd been there all along. I nodded at them like I'd known they were there the whole time. Behind me came a rustle of cloth as another boy ducked behind a line of wash. Apparently, word traveled fast when someone new showed up.

"So then . . . ," said the boss kid. "You an Okie. You new here. And you nosey. All right . . . What I can't tell," he went on, sliding his thumb along his jaw, "is whether you a ballplayer or not."

Wild horses sprang up inside me and it was all I could do to hold still and say, "Sure am."

I waited for the hoots, I waited for the hollers, but it was as silent as a ghost town. Boys hiding behind lines of wash edged quietly closer, eyes darting between me and the kid with the ball.

Finally, what looked like a smile broke across his face.

"Well, you got moxie, that's for sure," he said. "We in an interesting situation. 'Cause we down a guy on our team. Suppose this might just be your lucky day."

The world went gold, and the wind in the trees started singing my name.

"Just so happens I'm down a team," I said, which was true, and then I added, "I played with the all-star Balko boys back home the past three seasons," which wasn't.

Oh well.

The air was still for a minute until the first shutterbug of the evening gave a chirp like he was cheering me on. Some of the boys were grinning and creeping closer like it was safe to come out now that the baseball kid had called this my lucky day.

"Can you run fast?" called a boy behind the wash.

"Sure can."

"Can you think quick?" asked another.

"You bet."

"How's your throw?" asked the tall boy with the bat.

All the shutterbugs were singing together now and my grin was wider than a prairie.

"How 'bout you let me come show you what I got?" I said, my arm itching and tingling.

There was a whoop and a holler that spiraled out around me. This was a show now, and I was the main attraction. Only the boss kid held his place and held my gaze. He was the key to this whole operation and his poker face was better than any I'd seen in a picture.

"I guess we can try you for outfield," he said, running his thumb over the ball's red stitching.

The horses in me were rearing up, ready to bust out into a gallop. "Outfield ain't exactly my *position*," I fired back. "Outfield's a dime a dozen. Me? I *pitch*."

The air went cool and the smiles on the boys' faces dropped to the ground. The boss kid took a step towards me, holding his arms out like he was gathering the sky.

"Oh, you a *pitcher*, huh?"

His poker face was cracking just a bit and I couldn't tell why.

"I am," I said, "I got a mean whip, too. I can spin it, curve it, hook it, you name it."

The words came out like dancing ponies, and I was roping them around and around.

"Well," said the boss kid, turning back to his crowd. "We already got a pitcher."

"Well, lemme go up against him," I said.

"Nah," he said.

"Well, why not?"

He shot me a look that burned.

"'Cause you ain't worth my time."

He winked. So *he* was the pitcher. Well then. No wonder he'd gone all prickly.

"Why don't you go on home?" he said.

I'd heard that before, a hundred, maybe a thousand times. Maybe it was the size of the sky above me, or maybe it was the purple lip of a mountain I could just see off in the distance, but I wasn't going home. Not without a fair chance at playing.

"Not on your life," I said under my breath.

"What'd you say?" he called back.

A little wind swelled behind me like applause.

"I *said*, I'll bet your bottom dollar I *am* worth your time! Put me up against your best batter, I'll strike him out. Set me a target, I'll hit it. Shoot, I bet I could knock that cap right off your head if you held still enough."

In front of me, every mouth was hanging open like I'd just roped a wild horse.

The boy shook his head and laughed, a little too loud. "Ain't no way I'm letting a noodle-armed girl throw a baseball at my *head*."

"You scared I could do it?" I shot back.

"I'm scared you might knock my teeth out."

The boys were watching so hard they should've had popcorn.

"All right," I went on, "what you think you got on me? I can hit an apple out of a tree, a bird out of the sky—"

"Sure you can," he sassed back.

"Shoot, I had hitters break bats, I threw so hard!"

"That's a load of baloney—"

"And back in Oklahoma, I near got thrown in the clink for throwing a rock through a bank man's windshield from a hundred feet away!"

Behind him, a delicious chorus of hums and almost-cheers rose up into the air.

"Did you break it?" someone called.

"Sure did!"

"Did you bust it up real good?"

"Shoot!" I said. "Cracked it right down the middle."

There was an explosion of claps and whistles.

"Listen up!" spat the kid with the ball. "I told you to get on home. And I don't like repeating myself."

A kid with a sunburn blazing across his cheeks shifted from one foot to the next. "Eh, c'mon now, ain't no harm seeing what she's got," he said.

A few of the boys nodded, and the world went gold again.

"Might be good," another one said, "just to see. I—I ain't making no promises, but we can *see*."

I could've cartwheeled, danced.

Quentin tossed his head back to the boy with the baseball.

"It'd be *strategic*," he said. "A *strategic* tryout, since—"

"Since what?"

Something had fallen over the boss kid's face, like a shadow.

"Since *what*?" he said again, his voice slicing through the air.

Quentin was silent. But I knew he wanted to see what I could do. They all did. And there were more of them than *him*.

"Y'all listen up," he called. "You ever seen a skirt on a team? Huh? Have you? A *skirt*?"

The word pumped a jolt into the air. Some of the boys shook their heads. All of them were listening. His words were a trap, to make me mad, to watch me go wild. I let them glance off me and held my ground.

"That's right," he went on. "You ain't never seen a skirt on a team, because it just ain't *professional*. Lemme lay this out for you, there some sound reasons ain't no skirts on no teams. One, they ain't got the *disposition*. You want a teammate of yours to cry 'cause she's scared of losing?"

It was a stupid, easy thing to say and it wasn't even true. But a few of the boys nodded. Suddenly I could smell the toilets again.

"*Two*," he went on, "skirts ain't good at keeping secrets. You know that, I know that. We tell her where the field is and who we play, she gonna go blabbing to her friends."

It stung like a switch. I didn't even have anyone to blab to. And now more of them were nodding, collecting around him and marching to the beat of his words. The boss kid was like a song that everyone hummed along to. They *listened* when he talked. The tether between me and them had gone slack. They were pulling away, and they were going fast.

"*But*," he said, raising his arms. "This is a democracy, so I guess we put it to a vote."

He was going to make it seem like it was their idea to keep me out after they'd been ready to let me in. This was worse than Balko.

"All in favor of trying a *girl* out, say *aye*."

He'd lingered on that word "girl" as long as he could. Around me, the boys all held their tongues. I saw Quentin open his mouth like he was about to say *aye,* then dart his eyes to his friends, and hold back.

The boss kid shrugged.

"Looks like there's no room for skirts on this team, *girlie*."

I felt my jaw pull in tight like a fiddle string and my lungs fill up with hot, dry air. "You ought to watch your mouth. My name's Gloria."

The boy spat again and whistled.

"You kind of a poor excuse for a skirt anyway. You ugly as sin."

A blast of heat spread across my chest where the words had lashed out, and I hated that he'd gotten to me. And then there was laughing. In front of me, to my left, to my right, and worst of all, from behind me.

"Well," he said with another shrug that made me want to run up and kick him, "I guess we seen all we need to see here."

And he turned to go, all the boys falling in line at his back, leaving me there with words pounding in my skull and fire shooting down my limbs. As they walked, they talked, and I didn't have to hear what they were saying to know it was about me. And then the kid with the ball looked over his shoulder with a mean little smile and said something under his breath that made the others burst out laughing.

So that was how it was. Didn't matter how good you were. They'd find a way to keep you back and call it fair. Call you ugly while they were at it. Jess was right. *Ain't no group of boys ever gonna let a girl play ball with them,* she had said. And now they were laughing at me. Laughing at me and walking away. I was full of fire, crackling and popping, about to split me down the middle.

My hand shot down to the ground to the nearest stone, I swung it back over my shoulder, took a quick run to add speed to my throw, aimed squarely at the new boy's sideways cap, and then—

He saw what I was about to do, whistled, and gave a toothy smile.

Like he was *pretending* to be impressed.

Might as well have punched the wind right out of me.

My stone hit the ground behind me with a *thud* and my face went fire-hot.

The kid shook his head and motioned for the others to follow him.

"Like I said, ain't got the disposition," he said, just loud enough for me to hear before turning the corner and leaving me alone with the shanties and the fences and a little cabin that wasn't even partly mine.

Chapter Eight

Number 72 looked about as miserable as you'd expect. Maybe it *was* the same as the hundreds of other shacks, but ours just looked sadder, with its darkened door, its sagging porch, and the smell of disinfectant rolling off it. Staying here felt a thousand times sorrier than sleeping under the stars.

Pa caught my eye as he hoisted a crate of Ma's cooking things up into his arms.

"What you looking at? You gonna help?" he snapped.

"Yessir," I said, and pulled a soft sack out of the back. I wasn't even sure why we were unpacking since we wouldn't be here long anyway. Sooner we moved on, I figured, the better. This place stank and there wasn't a nice fella anywhere I could see.

I followed Pa into the shanty and the world went dark. I stood for a moment at the door waiting for my eyes to adjust. It was a single room with a small cooking stove in the corner. The floor sagged a bit in the middle and the small window in front was cloudy and cracked. In the middle of the floor, Pa had unrolled the mattress that me and Jess slept on. My baseball was lying on top. Pa must have tossed it there. I shoved it under the pillow so I didn't have to see it staring up at me.

"This place ugly as sin," I said.

Pa dropped the crate with a clatter and whipped around.

"This place ain't fine enough for you?" he demanded.

"I didn't say that."

"Nah, you don't have to. It's written all over your face."

I lowered my gaze. Last thing I needed was for Pa to be angry at me. He stood there, breathing hard from the weight of everything he'd lifted, until he waved me away.

"Just go on and have a seat outside. You not gonna help, stay out of my way."

I didn't need to be told twice.

Out front, I slumped on the steps praying one of those boys wouldn't come walking by and make some comment about my *disposition*. Maybe this place was big enough that I could just disappear into the trees. But if I had to bet, I knew I'd be seeing them all over.

From the porch I could smell scorched cooking smoke. When the wind blew a certain way, the hot stink of the johns came knocking at my nose. It was better than the smell of disinfectant inside the cabin. Smelled like they'd doused the whole place in bleach.

The last few folks were coming in from the orchard and walking to their cabins, a sea of grays and browns. They were rubbing red eyes and dragging their feet. Every once in a while, I caught the tail end of a mean joke or the sharp sound of a cussword. And then just beyond them I saw a soft blush of pink.

A girl not much older than Jess was sitting on her own steps across the way, faded dress fluttering around her ankles. Her man was standing next to her, smoking down the last drag of a cigarette. I couldn't tell if he was the boney type, or if he'd just gone hungry too many nights in a row. The two of them were staring at a baby boy the girl was bouncing in her lap. He let out a long thin howl and sent his arms high in the sky, fingers spread wide. The girl whispered something sweet into her arms and loosened the top of her dress as she cooed.

This was a rotten place to be a baby. Too crowded, too smelly, too mean. Maybe it was good Little Si hadn't made it to California. And just then the girl looked up and half smiled at me.

I looked away and pretended I didn't see, even though she'd caught my eye.

The creak of Pa's step sounded behind me and he dropped a pail next to me. "You go get some water for your ma."

"Yes, sir," I said, grateful for a chance to walk away. Grateful to not see Ma return and have to look at a baby that had made it to California.

I made my way to the camp water pump, keeping my head down as much as I could without tripping. The pump stood in a sea of mud that squished beneath my feet. When the bucket was full, I stepped carefully through the muck, water sloshing over and leaking into my boots.

"California, you are a bust," I said out loud, which was easier than saying I felt rotten.

"Hey, you there," a wiry little voice called out.

I turned to see a half-naked little boy leaning so far out a window he looked like he was about to take flight. His hair was white-blond, and his face was brown with freckles.

"You just got here," he said. "I saw you running for the john."

"Yeah, well," I muttered. I was sure making a first impression on the Santa Ana Holdsten Peach Orchard.

"You know," the kid said, his voice singsongy and fine, "Terrance won't let me play with him, neither. On account of my being small."

"Terrance?"

"Terrance Bowman. Runs the place—well, the boys anyway. Ain't got a nice bone in his body."

I didn't have to ask to know who he was talking about. Just thinking about him made me wish I had thrown that stone. Knocked the cap right off his head. I could have done it.

"Aw, don't blame him for being mean. His ma ran off with a traveling man . . . that's what I heard."

"Huh," I said.

"Psst," the kid went on, and he leaned his little body even farther out the window and beckoned me closer with a skinny little arm.

"Yeah . . . ?"

The kid's eyebrows raised up. "Can you keep a secret?"

"Sure," I said. As long as someone was offering.

The kid balanced his hips on the windowsill and cupped his hands around his mouth even though there was no one around.

"Those boys get licked real good by the apricot team every Sunday. *Every Sunday.*"

My ears perked up. "Apricot team?"

"Michelson's," the kid said, whispering as loud as he could. "Michelson's Apricot Grove. They got their own team, and we got ours."

"Why you whispering?" I whispered back.

"'Cause we ain't supposed to be consorting with them."

I couldn't imagine why people who picked peaches couldn't *consort* with people who picked apricots.

"Why the heck not?" I asked.

"Don't want us talking."

"Talking 'bout what? Picking fruit?"

"Talking 'bout wages, mostly. My cousin's over there. I see him after picking's done. But we don't talk about wages anyway. Mostly we play bottle caps." The kid leaned back against the windowsill and swung his skinny leg in the air. "It's true you play for a real team back in Oklahoma?"

I looked him up and down. I had at least a few years on him and I wasn't sure what he meant by a "real team," but I figured if anyone was going to believe a lie like that, it was a little kid hanging out a window wanting to talk baseball.

"Sure did," I said. The lie made me feel half good again.

"Well," he said, "them apricots got a batter that no one can strike out, name's Arlon Mackie. I ain't never heard of Terrance striking him out once. *Not once.* Anyhow, they practice across the creek on your way outta the camp. You want in? You small but not as small as me. You just follow the road on the way outta camp, turn at the big old climbing tree and follow the creek, that's where they'll be when they not picking."

His words sent a shiver of excitement through me. "They play ball when they're supposed to be *picking?*"

The kid grinned and whispered, "Yeah!"

I'd filched extra biscuits.

I'd thought about baseball in church when I was supposed to be thinking about God.

But I'd *never* ducked work when a crop had to come in.

"How you get out of camp without being noticed?" I asked.

"You gotta head out when you hear the warden's radio program come on. *Dick Tracy*, that's what he likes, copper show. He's just sitting in his office, ain't thinking about nothing else but Dick Tracy."

"How you know so much?"

The kid shrugged. "I keep an eye out and an ear to the ground. You need to know something, you

come to me! Just don't be wandering around aft
wards. Only thing bosses hate more than us eatii
peaches or bruising peaches is vagrants. You can g
thrown in the clink for that."

I peered into his face, trying to tell if he was my
age and just awful small, or younger than me and
talking beyond his years. "What do you know about
the clink and vagrancy?"

"I know plenty 'cause my daddy been in when
they stopped him for being out too late and he
didn't have a nickel."

I nodded slow. He said it like it was nothing.

"Hey, listen, if you tell a soul it was me who told
you 'bout Arlon and how Terrance can't strike him
out," he went on, his whisper turning into a fierce
rushing thing, "I will swear on a stack of Bibles I
didn't."

I leaned in close. "I won't tell. I promise."

The kid nodded, and quick as a wink, pulled
himself back through the window, then hitched one
leg over it to swing in the air. I peered into the dark
house behind him. "Where's your ma?"

He shrugged. "I dunno."

"And your pa?"

He squinted off in the distance. "Dunno that,
neither. Round somewhere I guess?"

That boy had lit a match in my brain, but I didn't

want a boy littler than me to feel more important than he was, so I looked casually over my shoulder. "Well, I gotta get home to mine. You got a name, fella?"

He leaned his tiny frame against the wood. "Sure do. Name's Davey. From the Bible."

I never heard of a "Davey from the Bible," but I nodded like I did and tipped my cap.

"Gloria," I said, and started walking back to number 72.

"Say," called Davey-from-the-Bible, "maybe if you make it on the team, you might let me practice with y'all sometime. I could be swell, I know I could. Even if I'm small. I'd work up to it, if you know what I mean."

I shrugged. "I guess," I said.

Those two words might as well have been a medal of honor. He was beaming. "And like I said, anything you need to know," he said again, "you ask me, ya hear?"

He was small there sitting in his window, full of big ideas and more gossip than a preacher's wife. I gave him a nod and headed back. The camp was still a sea of hunched shoulders and stinking laundry. I was sore from sitting in the truck all day and more than a little hungry, but what Davey had said made me feel like I sucked down a soda pop.

It was Terrance Bowman's team, and it was Terrance Bowman who was pitcher. It was Terrance who'd called me a skirt, and a girlie, who'd turned everyone against me. Terrance who'd made them all laugh at me.

But if what Davey-from-the-Bible said was true, it was also Terrance's fault they couldn't beat the boys over at Michelson's. Arlon Mackie, whoever he was, was too good for Terrance's throw. Maybe *that* was why he was so bent on making them laugh at me.

He was afraid I was just plain better than him.

Looking through the fence at those peaches, I figured we couldn't be here more than a couple weeks. That wasn't much time to wait around and hope Terrance and the rest of them would reconsider. And maybe all they wanted was to have a last couple games, Arlon Mackie or no.

Or maybe, what they really wanted was to *win*.

And maybe I was all they needed.

All I had to do was show them.

Well, all right then.

I was going to follow those boys the next day and strike them all out if I had to.

Whether Terrance Bowman liked it or not.

Chapter Nine

I woke up the next morning with the smell of disinfectant pricking at my nose and the idea of ducking work pricking at my brain. The thought of sneaking up on those boys had kept me staring up at the ceiling all night. Well, that and the baseball shoved under my pillow. It was delicious to dream about. But now I had to *do* it. I'd be lucky if I didn't come home tonight with a fresh shiner on my face.

For now it was just Jess's *feet* that were in my face. Beyond the thin flour-sack sheet me and Pa had hung up the night before, I could hear my parents rolling over and shaking the sleep out of their heads.

"Up and at 'em," Pa mumbled, crawling out in his undershirt.

I pulled my overalls on while Jess combed her hair out with her fingers. Ma had already lit the stove and was melting lard into a blackened pan. By God, I couldn't wait to eat something that wasn't a potato! I didn't care what it was, so long as it wasn't soft and covered in sprouting eyes.

Ma was mixing up clabber and flour for fritters, and the way they hissed when they hit the pan made me want to fall on my knees like I was at revival. I missed her biscuits. I missed her breads. I missed her green beans, fading but crisp in vinegar. I missed smoky bacon and golden, runny egg yolks. I missed her blackberry jams, dark and sweet enough to keep a smile on your face all night. As the fritters fried, I wondered what else she'd gotten from the company store besides flour. Maybe some butter for melting on top, or a thick slice of salty ham. Maybe she'd even gotten a tin of fruit in syrup. Or milk, a nice cold jar of it with cream to stir in on top.

"Eat up," Ma said softly.

She laid four tiny pan fritters with no fixings in front of us and poured what was left of the grayish melted lard back into the jar. I stared down at the tiny thing and looked up at Ma. Last time she had made these, they were the size of my palm and two for each of us. Last time she'd made these, we still had eggs from Yvette and Rosalina. Last time she'd made these, the sitting room still had a rocking chair in it.

"Go on now," she said with a smile that almost made me think she believed it.

"I thought we could buy on credit at the company store, Ma. Ain't they got more than flour?"

Jess pinched me. Hard.

And Ma just turned her back on my question, wiping her hands on a dish towel.

Jess leaned in close. "Company store charges four times what flour's worth," she whispered, "so now we owe 'em for the flour and we owe 'em for rent and we owe 'em for electricity and the—"

Snap!

Ma's dish towel whipped fiercely against her side, and Jess's words dried up right in her mouth. Whatever sunniness Ma was putting on went out through the cracks in the wood panel. She stood as still as a picture with the dish towel hanging from one hand. I watched the back of Ma's head to see what she would do next. But all she did was touch a finger to her temple and say quietly, "Eat up, girls." I listened for Pa to say something about us minding our ma, but he either wasn't paying attention or he had nothing to say about it.

"It's all right, Ma," Jess said. "I'll walk with you into town and we can see what they got there after picking's done. It's bound to be cheaper."

"Yeah" was all Ma said.

I popped the fritter in my mouth and counted to ten while I chewed. Best to make it last. Then I swept the crumbs from our little table into my hands, tossing them down the back of my throat, dust and all.

I was pulling on my boots when an announcement came over the speakers that had howled the morning alarm just moments before. Something about gathering at the gates before picking started, "camp-wide meeting" or something or other. For a moment I hoped there was some camp breakfast for all of us pickers, but by the look and feel of the place, they probably just had some talking to do to us.

Ma was still turned against the wall with her finger touching her temple and the dish towel hanging like a limp rag of surrender.

"Y'all go on ahead and pick," she said. "They need women in the cannery. I expect I'll be more useful there than up a tree."

So we went.

Me, Pa, and Jess walked through the rows of shanties towards the gates. I looked around as more and more people came out, some of them greeting each other like real neighbors. I wondered if they'd been here that long or if they were traveling together from back wherever they came from. Whoever they were, there were lots of them. There must have been millions and millions of peaches beyond the fence that separated the camp from the orchard.

I turned to Pa. "How many acres did we have? In Oklahoma, how many?"

Pa gave my shoulder a squeeze. "Doesn't matter," he said.

"Well, I wanna know."

"Seventy-five."

"And how many acres this place?"

Pa whistled. "I don't know. Didn't think one person could ever own so much."

I turned to Jess.

"Jess," I whispered.

"What."

"This place so big maybe you'll find Joe Franklin's sweet son here."

"Shut up, Gloria."

We turned a corner and then I saw it—an orchard. But this wasn't any old orchard like the ones in Oklahoma. This was like an entire *country* of orchard. Rows and rows of green-topped trees with little blushing fruits peeking out as far as the eye could see. It was like looking out over the prairie; there was no end of it. And the only thing between us and that prairie of peaches was the longest fence there ever was, glinting with barbed wire at the top.

The moving and the chatter around me stopped like a freight train coming to a tired halt. Up ahead was a gate that opened to the trees. Someone had set a little platform up and I watched as a round man in a fine white suit stepped up like he was going to speak. He wore a white hat to match that had a ribbon the color of plums around it. Behind him two men in white pants who held clipboards stood like guard dogs at the gate.

"Well, looky here," a man to my left said, eyeing the man with the white hat.

I turned to take a look at him. He was all salt and pepper with uneven whiskers and wrinkles deep enough to grow potatoes in. He caught me looking.

"You like hearing hogwash?" he asked.

I shrugged.

"Well, you're about to get an earful."

The man with the white hat cleared his throat.

"Good morning, ladies, gentlemen! I'm here as a representative of the California Growers Association to commend you on the fine job you are doing getting these peaches in. I always say, American workers are the best workers in the world, and what I see right here are *American workers!*"

He puffed out his chest and smiled on his last bit like he was expecting applause, but nobody moved.

"Now, you all are here because you are *fine American workers.* You are here because you want to *work.* Not like them folks coming up from the border and causing trouble. This may be the land of the free, but friends, this is not the land of the *free-loaders.*"

"That's right!" someone called.

A few pickers were nodding, but some of them were as still as fence posts.

He went on.

"And that's why we hire native-born Americans here. We are not going to have ourselves a *situation* like they had down in Fresno, no sir, we don't hire lowlifes. You want to work for a place that pays the same wages to you as to someone who doesn't speak English, or someone that thinks handouts are a way of life?"

He paused.

"Nope!" someone shouted.

"*Exactly.* You go on over to Michelson's if you want that. Not here, we hire good folk, country folk, Christian folk who believe in hard work and a little bit of sweat."

Folks around me were nodding, saying *That's right* under their breaths, and I almost wanted to say it with them. But I also got the funny feeling someone was yanking my chain. The man to my left was shaking his head. "Keep 'em fighting each other, never see it's the same man keeping 'em down."

The fellow next to him nodded his head in agreement.

"So," the man in white went on, "you can imagine how upset I was to hear about the *incident* last week causing trouble for you fine folk. Turns out, we were dealing with a snake. Told us he was decent. Told us he was like *you*. But he was nothing but a dirty Red."

The man to my left scoffed. "That's one way to put it," he said.

I shifted onto one foot. I was getting the sense something was going on here that had started long before we pulled up. Maybe Terrance and his team needed another player because one of the boys was an *outside agitator*, whatever that was. Maybe Jimmy from 72 was trouble. Or maybe his pa was.

"So I'm just here to say that we are grateful to have such fine people working in the best orchard in California and we will not stand for anyone to get between you and your *hard work*. You and your *wages*. Do I make myself clear?"

There was a bobbing of heads all around me.

"Well now, I know you are eager to get to work, and I will not keep you from it!" he sang out, and two men with clipboards went to unlock the gate to the peaches. I turned my face up to Pa.

"What's he driving at?" I asked.

Pa kept his gaze fixed on the man with the hat. "What he's driving at—at least, what I think he's driving at—is that he don't want no one stirring up trouble for us here."

"Trouble?"

"Getting you thinking someone owes you something. Complaining about wages, or getting organized."

The crowd started moving into the orchard.

"What do you mean, getting organized?"

"Causing trouble. Making nonsense. What folks do when they too lazy to put in an honest day's work."

"They scared we lazy?"

"They scared 'cause folks who ain't cut out for hard work been all over this valley. Driving down wages, then asking for more. Folks who ain't even American or don't know what America's about. Folks who skip town before paying rent."

He stopped and crouched to look me in the eye. "You and me ain't like that. We know what it's like to own what we pick. Picking someone else's fruit just one step towards getting our own land, hear me?"

"I hear you, Pa."

"You and me, we know we got to put in our time, give a little sweat, and we do it ourselves, we don't need anyone but us. That's how we get ahead, Gloria."

I stared right through him. "Ain't that what we done back home?"

Something broke in Pa's face and Jess elbowed me in the ribs.

"No, that's—Shoot, Gloria, I ain't got time to explain everything to you. Get on, go. You're a quick climber, so get on up one of those ladders and get the hard-to-reach ones, hear? Jess, go on and fetch some picking sacks."

Jess ducked away like she was trying to prove how hard she was listening, and Pa walked up towards a cluster of wheelbarrows.

I nodded and cast my gaze around for Terrance, or any of the other boys, but I was swimming in grown folks. Between the millions of peaches and the hundreds of pickers and the miles of fences, it didn't come as a surprise that eight scrappy boys could duck out for a bit.

I walked to the tallest tree I could find with a

grayish ladder leaning up into the highest branches.

"You watch yourself on those," came a voice that sound like it was wrung out of a dish towel. "These ladders ain't good for nothing but firewood."

It was the man with the wrinkles you could grow potatoes in. He came on over, looking at the ladder suspiciously. He reached out a knobby old hand and pulled hard on a few of the rungs.

"Halfway decent," he said. "Don't want you or no one falling. Saw a guy fall fifteen feet the other day, he was lucky enough to fall on his bum in a nice patch of grass."

"Hey, thanks!" I said, starting up the ladder. "Name's Gloria Mae Willard."

The man's lips curled up into a smile and his wrinkles became Arizona canyons.

"Grady," he said, and removed his hat, sending thin wisps of hair up into the sky. He handed me a picking sack and turned to go. I watched him walk on and saw that two of the clipboard men were watching him and whispering to one another.

I smiled.

Didn't know much about this place but I knew that Grady was playing for my team.

"Gloria, stop looking around, get a move on," said Jess. She had finished filling up her picking sack and was carefully stacking her peaches onto a wheelbarrow.

I wanted to drop a peach square on her head, but I'd already heard some of the clipboard men say they were docking someone's pay because they'd loaded up their cart until it was overflowing and spilled peaches out the side. Between Jess bossing me every which way and those clipboard men fussing and fuming, I'd already about had it with the Santa Ana Holdsten Peach Orchard.

Besides, there were better places to be than up a tree.

"Pssst," came a voice through the trees.

I looked through the leaves and saw two bright eyes fixed on mine from the next tree over. It was Davey-from-the-Bible, his little frame half hooked around the ladder and half around the branches. He was grinning and waving.

"Whatchu doing this far in?" he said. "You ain't gonna hear the copper show all the way over here. If you want to find them boys you gotta hug the fence, work the trees over by the main gate. Can't hear a lick of nothin' this far in."

Davey was talking like one of those kids who likes to show off what he knows. It didn't sit right by me. He'd said himself that Terrance wouldn't let him play, and that meant that all the other kids my size had already shaken him off. If I wasn't careful, I'd be the sucker he latched on to.

"I can't just leave," I said. "I got my pa watching me and my sister close."

Davey shrugged. "Duck, say you're going to the john, or you say one of those clipboard men asked you to get up high in another tree."

I eyed Pa. He was deep in the leaves, the wheelbarrow half full already, and Jess was halfway to the sorting house.

"Glo, you better go on," Davey said. "You gonna miss your chance to—"

"All right, hush up now," I snapped.

He was starting to annoy me. Especially the way he called me Glo like we'd known each other longer than we had. I had a good couple years on him, and I was beginning to think the boys on Terrance's team had put him off because he was small and annoying, not because he couldn't play.

Davey sighed and shrugged his shoulders. "Say, if you're not gonna go, you wanna come back with me when we done picking? I got a swell bottle cap collection. Fifty-four. Bottle caps, that is. I been saving the best ones. Got bottle caps from nine states. You wanna see?"

I ducked behind a branch so he couldn't see me as well. "Maybe later."

"Sure thing. So you gonna go play ball? You oughtta go if you gonna go."

"I'm gonna go."

"Say, you think I could come with? I won't ask to play or nothing—"

"No!"

It came out a little too fast. But I couldn't bring some little kid with me that was already barred from playing.

Davey got quiet in his tree. For a moment, I worried he was sore about me telling him no. But then his little tin-whistle voice came piping through the trees same as ever. "Well, if you change your mind, you let me know. Course I *could* go anytime I want."

"Sure you could," I whispered underneath my breath, and dropped down to the ground before Davey could ask me another question or even noticed I'd slipped away.

The trees near St. Peter's little booth were picked over and sorry-looking. Just a few straggling folks were picking there, making sure there wasn't any blushed yellow color poking out of the green. And then I heard it—a crackle and pop of a radio dial almost as soft as a fly buzzing against a window.

And then—

"Calling all adventure fans! Calling all *Dick Tracy*

fans! Stand by! *Dick Tracy* is on the air!"

Something shocked through the air. There was a rustle here, a snap of twig there. I crouched down low and listened to the sound of footsteps weaving in and out of the trees around me, heading for the gate. Peeping through the trees, I swore I saw the brown-black mop of Quentin's hair floating between the low-hanging branches. If I listened closely I could hear the occasional sharp whisper calling to "Hurry up!" and "Duck!"

I waited for it all to rustle on out of the trees. No point in blowing my cover and getting laughed back into camp. When I was sure no boy would catch me too close on their heels, I slipped out of the gate and walked alongside the big white entrance to the orchard. I could see into St. Peter's little booth, and sure enough, he was hunched over his radio set with his back turned to his little window. Beyond him was the wide-open gate to the world beyond.

Sneaking out would be as easy as pie.

I ducked down as low as I could go and snuck under the window to the sounds of Dick Tracy trying to get to the bottom of some ancient curse. It sounded like they were dealing with invisible ink and maybe even a stowaway. If I hadn't been itching to play ball, I would've sat there listening to find out how it all shook out.

But the wind beyond the gate was whispering my name, and the road that stretched out from camp was wide and golden.

In three quick strides I was out, slipping between delivery trucks for cover and breaking into a run down the path that Davey had mentioned, which would lead me to their field. All I had to do was figure out exactly what to say and do before I got there. All I had to do was—

"What's she doing here?"

Aw, shoot.

To my left was a big old climbing tree with a boy perched on every branch.

They'd seen me coming. And they'd been lying in wait.

And standing straight up on a branch like he'd lived up a tree his whole life was Terrance Bowman, fingers already curling into a fist.

Chapter Ten

"What are you doing here, and who told you how to find us?" Terrance said, dropping down from his branch.

I held my tongue. I needed to say the right thing, not the quickest thing.

"I'm here," I said very slowly, "to try out for your team. I'm here to pitch for one or all y'all."

I looked around at all of their bewildered faces and added, "I know you need someone. Ain't that right, fellas?"

I could feel jumping bugs bounding around my ankles, but I held still.

"Thought I told you yesterday, girl, we don't need no skirt on our team."

I breathed in the California air like it was courage. "My name ain't *girl*, it's Gloria, and you best remember that."

"You gimme one good reason why we shouldn't throw you out on your bum right now."

"I'll give you two," I said. All around me, the faces of the boys were burning bright and curious. All I had to do now was unwind them from Terrance's little finger so I could put them in my back pocket. If I played my cards just right, it might work.

"First off, you said yourself you need another player. You beggars who acting like you can choose."

"Who you calling beggar? Girl, you don't—"

"Second, *Terrance*, rumor has it you ain't been able to strike Arlon Mackie out. Not once. Rumor has it those apricot boys got you licked. As pitcher, that's on you."

The temperature dropped just then, along with Terrance's words. My toes dug into the soles of my boots, holding on for dear life. I was playing with fire and was probably going to get burned at least a little. But what I said was true. It was written all over the faces in front of me. It was in the way the boys' eyes darted to the ground. The way no one came to

Terrance's defense. And it was in the way Terrance's
fingers flexed and curled.

Maybe I would get that shiner after all.

I could take it.

"Who you been talking to?" he said slowly.

I whistled up to the sky to buy a little time.
Something told me mentioning Davey-from-the-
Bible would get me nothing but trouble. "I wouldn't
say I been talking to anyone, just seems like the
whole camp knows about it."

That sent a jolt through the boys. With one flick
of Terrance's hand, they began dropping down from
the tree and collecting at his back in faded jeans
and rope suspenders. They might have been curious about me, might have even given me a second
chance, but they were still Terrance's team. One
word from him and they'd be on me like a flock of
locusts. But he just stepped on closer till he was near
enough to throw a punch.

"Listen," Terrance said, "I'll say it again. Ain't
no *skirt* coming on this team."

I tipped forward at my hips so he could see the
look in my eyes just a little bit better. "Well, good
thing I got my overalls on."

A ripple of laughs sounded behind him. But this
time, they were laughing *with* me.

"Lord, you got a mouth."

"Boy, I got an arm."

"Girl, you ain't never playing for us, let alone *pitching* for us. I ain't stepping aside to get laughed at by Michelson's boys 'cause I let a skirt on."

"Well, what if that skirt could strike Arlon out? Who'd be laughing then?"

The air was thick and hot again and bursting with electricity. It was like one of those dust storms when the air was tingling and dangerous. I'd come ready to throw a baseball, but it looked like I was more likely to throw a punch.

"Gentlemen," called a voice that was clear and calm.

Terrance kept his eyes on me but turned his head slightly.

"What do you want, Quentin?"

A cool breeze broke the summer heat.

"I believe there is a way to settle this," Quentin said.

"I *believe* this girl could've blown our cover."

A few of the boys nodded.

"That's true," said Quentin. "She could've, but she didn't."

The boys all looked Quentin's way.

"What I propose," he said, "is a wager."

There was a stirring from the boys and I heard a few of them whispering under their breath.

"Aw, c'mon now!" Terrance scoffed, but from what I could tell, he was the only one that thought it was a rotten idea. All the others were pitched forward on their toes, eyes bright and watchful. I wasn't sure where this was going, but it suddenly seemed less likely to end in a busted lip.

Quentin looked my way. I'd never seen anyone turn an angry tide peaceful just with words. It was almost enough to make me let my guard down. Almost.

"Let's put her to the test. Set your terms and let her show us if she's any good."

He looked at Terrance and said softly, "We need one more since Jimmy went."

Terrance looked away like he didn't want to talk about it, or he didn't want me to see his face.

We were all under Quentin's spell, and I could see Terrance fighting it. But he was outnumbered. His breath was catching in his chest, like he was trying to come up with the right words to turn everyone mean and angry again. Quentin just watched calmly, like he'd seen Terrance wild and mad a million times.

I watched him, too, as he shifted from one foot to another, setting his jaw and then swallowing hard. He turned away and went back to the group of boys behind him. He pulled one of the boys to the side.

It was the tall kid who'd held the bat the day before. The edges of their whispers hissed through the air, but I couldn't make out the shape of their words. Finally Terrance whipped around and walked right at me, stopping close enough where I could feel his breath.

"Wager's on," he said. "Conditions is, you go up against our best batter. You gotta strike him out in three. No balls. No fouls. No wild pitches. Three honest-to-God strikeouts."

A smile burned at the edges of my mouth.

"Or?" I demanded.

"Or you leave us alone. You don't come near this field, and you don't talk to us round the orchard, or in the camp."

"And?"

"I wash your lying mouth out with soap."

That sounded awful.

"Fine!" I shouted.

"Well, all right!" Terrance shouted back a little too quickly.

"And if I strike him out?"

"Then I'm a Rockefeller."

"Terrance . . . ," Quentin said gently.

Terrance set his jaw hard and said, "If you strike him out, you can play on the team."

The smile broke across my face and I didn't care if I looked a fool.

"But listen up, you ain't *never* pitching for us, no way. That's *my* position, this *my* team."

A rush of fight flooded my head, but Quentin held up his hand.

"That, I believe, is what you'd call a compromise," Quentin said.

"Yeah, well—" I started.

"And a good *sportsman* would accept."

I wanted to tell them no deal. Swagger on up and throw the wager in Terrance's face. But that was what he wanted me to do. Show them I didn't have the *disposition* to play ball. Maybe all I needed was a foot in the door and then I could worry about flinging it wide open.

"I got a condition, too," I said.

"Name it," said Terrance.

"I ain't playing right field. Everyone knows that's where you stick someone you think is no good."

Quentin raised his hand. "Well, Gloria, right field's taken. That's my position."

I whipped around to face him.

"Quentin, I—"

He waved his hand and smiled. "I wouldn't have it any other way."

He stepped back and opened his arms up wide.

"All right now," he said, "you all heard the terms, time to shake on it."

I spat into my hand and held it out to shake. Terrance eyed me down his nose, but then walked up and spat a big one into his palm and we shook on it, eye to eye.

"All right, Gloria," said Terrance. "Time to show us what you got."

The boys fanned out in a circle around me. Back at the California border, I'd practiced my throw in the long, lonely hollow between two rocky slopes. It'd been quiet there, just me and the shutterbugs and the call of turkey vultures picking off whatever they were picking off. It'd been like something out of a cowboy movie, just me, with my eye on the target, and my arm aching and tingly from throwing so hard, eyes narrowed towards the setting sun. This was nothing like that.

Those boys were almost dancing around me, shouting and laughing and clapping. Terrance raised his fingers to his lips and whistled loud enough to break glass. The boys nodded and cocked their heads to one side. They sure shut up fast when he called.

"Girl's got three throws. No balls. No fouls. One of ours hits the ball, she gets her filthy, lying mouth washed out with soap, and I'm gonna be the one doing the washing."

The boys nodded, taking their places around me like they'd bought tickets to see it all go down.

"All right now," said Terrance, tossing me a look, "let's get this over with."

He'd said it like he didn't care. *Too* much like he didn't care. But there was a prick of panic in his voice that I could hear clear as day. He was afraid he wouldn't be able to put me off a second time.

"I said let's get this over with, huh, fellas?" he called. But no one was paying him any mind. They were watching me to see if I could take their batter down, whoever he was. The panic in Terrance's voice went right to his eyes as he looked around for someone to holler back that we ought to get this over with, but no one did.

This was my game now.

Terrance cupped his hands around his mouth. "Clyde!" he shouted.

Clyde stepped forward. He was the kid who'd been holding the baseball bat the day before. He had arms near as thick as those of a grown hay-baling man. He basketed his hands and flipped them around till his knuckles cracked. Even though I couldn't see all the boys, standing as they were all around me, I could feel each one of their smiles on my back. I knew some of them were hoping I'd fail so they could take me down to the creek and make me chew on soap flakes. Shoot, I might have hoped the same thing if I were in their shoes.

Lordy.

Clyde plucked what looked like the side of an old fruit crate out of the dirt and dropped it where he wanted it for home plate. He must've stood a whole head taller than most of the boys, not to mention me. He tapped the bat once to the plate and then swung it up over his shoulder. He nodded his head at me and took a deep breath.

Everyone was watching now.

"Catch," I heard a voice call softly. I turned to see Quentin with a baseball in his hand. I nodded and he threw it to me. Just threw it. Didn't launch it like he was trying to bust my head open, or toss it off to the side for me to run after. Just threw it. I caught it easy. *Thanks,* I mouthed. He nodded at me and took a few steps back.

"Go on, Casey," Quentin said, and the boy who looked like he'd baked too long in the sun squatted down behind Clyde with a busted-up catcher's mitt.

I turned the ball over in my hand. It was warmed from the sun and smelled like dog and dirt. For a moment I wished I'd brought my Texas ball with me, but knowing this crowd, they might run off with it, or throw it in a muddy pond somewhere if Terrance told them to.

"C'mon!" Terrance shouted at me. "Let's get this over with, ain't got all day!"

If that was supposed to throw me off, it didn't. I felt my whole body tighten up against Terrance's words and I saw a flash of nervousness in Clyde's eyes. I just smiled and wound my arm back like I'd done so many times in Oklahoma and sent the ball flying with my whole body wanting to just go along with it through the air. In a split second I saw Clyde's back arch as his bat whipped a ring around and—

THUNK!

The sound was glorious as the ball hit the old leather and sent a burst of dust up from Casey's mitt! All the boys around me let out a gasp.

Terrance just stood there.

Casey the catcher looked up at me, raised his eyebrows, and nodded, throwing the ball back in a smooth arc. I caught it easily and smiled back at him.

One down. Two to go.

The circle of boys had stepped in. Maybe a couple of them thought me getting a strike on Clyde was just good luck knocking twice. But I could see most of them were thinking maybe I *was* as good as I said. And maybe Terrance didn't know what he was talking about when it came to pitching. Maybe he wasn't even the right guy for the job.

I popped the ball into my left hand to let the blood rush all the way through my right, just to make sure it was in top-notch condition. I looked back to Clyde. His face had become fixed and focused. He was aiming to hit that ball hard and not lose any time thinking he didn't have to fight for it.

I breathed out slow and kept my eye on him.

THUNK!

The sound hit before Terrance could even open his mouth to tell me to hurry up.

Casey threw his mitt off like it was burning him and shook his hand while Clyde looked from the ball to me, from me to the ball like he could hardly believe he'd missed again. The rest of the team was wide-eyed, shaking their heads, and some of them were beaming. Some of them, maybe even most of them, wanted me to win this bet now. Some of them were rooting for me, deep down inside, I could feel it. Quentin was smiling, teeth and all.

Casey threw the ball to me like we were on the same team. Like he wanted me to catch it. And I did, and he nodded and he crouched down again, slipping the big dusty old mitt over his hand.

Two down.

One to go.

And if I missed?

Down to the creek and slimy soap in my teeth, and maybe even a kick in the ribs.

Laughing behind my back, boys whispering

"girlie" all around me and having to hang out with Davey for the rest of harvest.

And no baseball.

Just cooking, and picking, and scrubbing, and hoping.

Wanting it so bad was making me lose my nerve. I was damp all over and I felt the ball slip in my clammy hands. All around me, the boys were leaning in, aching to see if I could prove Terrance wrong.

"Go on, Gloria," I heard Quentin call softly.

Okay, I mouthed back at him.

I took a breath and looked into Clyde's eyes. He was gripping the bat so tight I could make out the bones in his hands. He was worried, and for a moment I felt bad for him for being the reason Terrance might lose his wager.

But never mind that.

I planted my feet in the earth, wound the ball back behind my ear, said a prayer, and—

"Hold up, wait a minute!" cried Terrance.

My right arm seized up and Casey and Clyde looked like they'd been jolted out of a dream.

Terrance strode up between me and home plate. "You need to think about this. Think about what it's gonna look like showing up with *her* playing for us."

"C'mon now, Terrance," said one of the boys. "Let her finish!"

But Terrance wasn't hearing it. "They gonna laugh at us!" he shouted. "They gonna think less of us! That what you wanna be? A joke?"

"Ain't gonna be a joke if we beat them apricots!" Casey called.

"You shook on it, Terrance," Quentin said.

"So what if I did? So what if I—"

He stopped midsentence, looking to the boys to see what they would do. But they didn't say anything. They wanted me to finish as much as I did. They didn't even care if I got the third strike.

"So that's *it*?" he cried. "Y'all fine with this? Don't y'all remember? She was *this close* to knocking me in the skull—"

"I was aiming for your cap, dummy!" I shouted. "And I would've hit it if I wanted, too!"

"Terrance!" called Quentin.

"Maybe I should've!" I shouted. "You trying to change the rules now you afraid I got you beat!"

"You trying to make a fool of me!"

"Well, you making it easy!"

"Terrance!" Quentin cried again as Terrance started running at me. I dropped the ball.

"Terrance Bowman!"

I didn't know how to fight. I didn't even know how exactly to surrender in a situation like this.

"Copper coming!"

Terrance froze. Everyone did like someone had thrown a pail of water on them. And like a flock of birds they all made for the piney bushes at the edge of the road.

I stood in place, not knowing if this was some kind of trick. Then I heard whispering coming from the bushes. *"Gloria, Gloria, Gloria! Get down, hide!"* I didn't know who was hissing it, but it didn't sound like a trick. It sounded scared. I ran towards the voices and a hand reached out and tugged me into the brush. Just then something came rolling around the curve in the road.

It was a police truck, the kind with room in the back for people, and it was slowing down, heading straight for the gates of the Santa Ana Holdsten Peach Orchard.

Chapter Eleven

The engine of the police truck shuddered off and St. Peter came out from behind the gate, white suit blinding in the sun. I guessed *Dick Tracy* was over now.

I touched my hand to my pocket. I didn't have a nickel, and I wondered if kids could get locked up for vagrants just like Davey's pa. Suddenly I wished I were still up a peach tree picking with everyone else.

"What's going on—"

"Shh!" came all the other voices at once.

The boys had all gone still and silent. Only the breeze rustled their hair.

I watched as two blue-clad policemen got slowly

out of the truck. They pulled their clubs out as they walked up to the man in white. And for one ridiculous moment I hoped they were there to take him away on account of him being so mean. But the three of them stood nodding like friends, and the man in white pointed back to the camp.

And then I heard shouting and struggling and I knew whoever they were coming for was on the other side of the gate.

The policemen cocked their heads towards the sound. I could make out the cusswords now that were ripping through the air. And there came a man, twisting and writhing with three men in white holding him and shoving him. He was spitting and covered in dirt like he'd been thrown down, and held down.

It was Grady.

The three men in white nodded at each other and then tossed him forwards with all their might. He stumbled and fell and made a move to scramble up, but before he could—

Thunk! came one of the clubs on the back of Grady's skull.

The sound carved a hollow space in my chest. It sounded like throwing a pumpkin against a stone, soft and hard at the same time. And wet. Grady kept on struggling up, dazed-looking, but still determined to get to his feet. Red sliced through his dirty skin and red came away on his hand when he touched his face.

My fingers were clawing into the dirt, back and forth. Dust filled my palms and I ground the little rocks into the soft of my hands to keep from leaping up and running or screaming out. I could hear the quickening of everyone's breath around me as we watched the policemen hoist Grady up and heave him into the back of the truck like a sack of grain.

I could hear him beating his fists against the sides, all muffled cusswords and boiling rage.

When the truck drove off, everyone was a little too still and a little too silent. The hopping bugs were laying low now, too, and the grasses had stopped singing to the trees. My mouth was on dry fire.

"Just like with Jimmy," Terrance said through his teeth.

The boys all nodded.

"They did that *to a kid*?" I said.

"Nah," said Terrance, "to his pa. Roughed him up so good, said his ma screamed when they let him out of the station."

"But why?"

"'Cause he was a Red," Terrance said, "said he was anyway."

"What's a Red?" I asked.

Different answers shot out of everyone's mouth.

"Someone who ducks work—"

"Guys who ain't American—"

"Someone who's trying to earn more—"

"Fella who causes trouble—"

"Someone who organizes—"

There was that word again. Sitting in a whole mess of other ones.

Quentin cleared his throat. "Strictly speaking, it's what they call us when they think we're complaining too much, be it about wages, or company store prices, or when your eyes burn from the spray. Or when you talk to someone else about any of that."

The boys chewed on it for a bit and then nodded, as if Quentin's definition held a little truth for all of them.

"Jimmy's father got to saying we should walk out. Not pick the peaches till they paid us a full twenty-five cents an hour. Went so far as to get ten other men to stop picking."

"But if you don't pick," I said slowly, "you don't get any money at all . . ."

Quentin nodded. "That's true, but see, the fruit keeps on going whether or not we pick it. And if we don't pick it, the fruit ripens and falls and gets soft. And then it's the guys that own the farm that lose out. If they're scared of that, of losing a whole bunch of money, then they gotta pay us more."

The boys had all quieted and had turned towards Quentin. They were listening with their heads on their knees, their arms pulling tightly across their shins.

Quentin went on. "And so, when they saw Jimmy's pa wasn't alone anymore, when he was making plans with others, they called the police and dragged him out by his shirt collar and then . . . it was pretty much like you just saw."

"Maybe a little bit worse," said Terrance quietly. His face had gone soft like he was watching the whole thing over again in his mind.

I looked to the spot where Grady had fallen and thought about what the man in the white suit had said about there being an incident last week.

"We should've stood up to them," Terrance murmured. "We shouldn't've let them do something like that to Jimmy's pa."

The boys were hanging their heads now. All that excitement and anger had slipped out and something like shame had crept in. Up ahead, St. Peter lit a cigarette and walked back into his little booth.

"Come on now," Quentin said quietly. "We gotta get in. If this is like last time, they'll be coming back with more."

We all looked to the gate.

"Who's gonna go first?" asked Casey.

No one said anything.

"I'll go," said Terrance.

In a strange sort of way, I was grateful.

We slipped in, one by one, bending low down so St. Peter couldn't see us from his chair. Normally this would've been the kind of thing that felt like an adventure, but I didn't feel too good after watching that man bleed. And I sure didn't feel like asking about where I stood with the team. As I crouched down, passing under the window, I heard St. Peter talking on the phone, deep and low with words like "Uh-huh" and "You bet" and "Yessir." Hadn't thought there'd be anyone above him to answer to, but I guess everyone's got someone to call sir, even if you're the one choosing who gets to work and who has to move on.

Once inside, we scattered. Something was different, though, and as I raced through the rows of trees looking for Jess, I could feel everyone keeping their heads down a little bit more than usual. The men with the clipboards seemed to have doubled since the morning and they were twitchy and pacing.

I found Pa hoisting a load of those hard yellow peaches on the back of a pickup. His collar was dark with sweat and his sleeves were rolled up as far as they could go.

When he saw me he almost dropped the load. His arms shot out and pulled me in close. He spoke in a fierce whisper.

"Where you been, Glo? I been looking all over for you! *Jess* has been looking all over for you!"

"I—" I started, not sure of what lie I should tell. Pa's eyes were frantic.

"Pa!" I heard Jess call, and I spun around to see her racing towards me.

She ran up, breathless, and Pa crouched down, one hand gripping my shoulder and the other hand gripping Jess's.

"Now, listen, both of you, we gotta stick together, all right? Jess, you don't let Gloria out of your sight, you hear?"

Jess was nodding and I was gawping and Pa was talking like the ground was about to split open underneath us.

"Listen, I gotta know where you are, you can't be wandering off, we gotta—"

"Problem here?"

The long shadow of one of the men with the clipboards fell across us and Pa jumped up, startled.

"No, sir," he said quick. "Just making sure I got my girls close, that's all."

"Well, that's just fine," said the man, with a smile that was too nice and too wide.

Pa had stood and turned back to the truck, nearly leaping into it to push the bushel of peaches back as far as it could go. He busied himself best he could. The man with the clipboard watched him do it and then walked on. When he had gone, Pa's shoulders fell. He looked at Jess.

"I'm gonna stay out till the sun starts setting. You get Glo home, help your ma with dinner, or the wash, or whatever needs doing. Don't talk to nobody, understand?"

Jess nodded. She was pink all over from the sun, her dress limp with sweat, her hem dirty and poor-looking.

"I understand, Pa," she said. "Let's go, Gloria."

I followed her through the rows of trees, listening to the strange sound of pickers not talking. She stared straight ahead, but I knew she had something up her sleeve.

"Where. Were. You," she finally said, slow, even, and low.

The air had cooled and a dark blue tint was coming across the sky. I heard the rumble of pickups getting ready to make their last delivery trips to the sorting house and the cannery.

"Picking," I lied. The word made my mouth go

dry. Jess never took an easy fib for an answer. She let the silence grow between us, which should have given me time to think of something better to say. But it didn't.

Ahead of me I could see the edge of the chain link fence that separated the orchard from the shanties. That man with the toothpick from the day before was standing there watching us walk. I shoved my hands in my pockets, wondering if he was going to make that kissy noise again or if he was going to be decent. Beside me, Jess quickened her pace. Just as we were passing he called out, "See you found your sister."

She nodded quickly but didn't slow down.

"Curfew in effect now," he went on. "No one out the front gate after eight, you hear that, missy?"

Jess stopped and looked at him. "But I gotta head into town."

"You get back here by eight o'clock, don't care where you go. But no way you making it to town and back before eight."

"We gotta get food—"

"We got food here. You need something? You go to the company store. You go on and tell your momma." He paused and then said, "You want, I can take you there myself."

I looked over my shoulder to see if Pa was

coming along behind us. He wasn't.

"No sir, I know my way around," said Jess.

He grinned. "Sure you do."

The way he said it was ugly. It made me glad I was swimming in dusty overalls. I reached up and pulled my cap down a little like it might help keep his funny little stares and smiles out. And I waited for Jess to say something. Something about minding his own business. Something sharp and sassy.

"We gotta be going," Jess said, taking me by the arm.

The man smiled so big I could see his teeth. "Well, go on. Pick up a nice can of Holdsten peaches while you're at it," he added, which made the policeman laugh.

Jess yanked me away from the two men chuckling. They were laughing at us. Well, they were laughing at *her*. I could tell she knew it because she was walking hard, kicking up dust behind her, each step angrier than the last. I felt hollow inside as the chuckling got softer behind us.

As soon as we were out of sight and earshot of the two men, I tugged Jess's hand as hard as I could.

"Why you ain't say nothing about that man talking nasty to you?"

Jess tugged me back hard, making me trip and stumble. "You mind yourself, Gloria. I'll mind me."

"Yeah, but—"

"Yeah but what?"

"It ain't right!"

"Maybe not, Glo, but it's just the way it is."

That was her answer for everything that was unfair. Everything she didn't have an answer to.

"Well, I think you oughtta—"

Jess whipped around, her face red and furious.

"I was looking for you," she burst out. "Right after it happened, I looked everywhere. I asked everyone, even *that* lousy son of a gun. Now where were you?"

"Picking," I said, the lie getting stronger and more dangerous. "And what are you talking about? After *what* happened?"

Jess started walking again, this time even faster. Probably to just keep me on my toes.

"I don't know where your head was buried, or what you was up to."

"What are you *talking* about?" I asked again.

"Word came round they were gonna cut wages, that they'd been planning on it. Twenty cents down to eighteen. And someone asked if that meant rent was going down, too. And they said no. And some of the men got to yelling, and then some of them got to fighting. And that man Grady climbed up a tree, and started talking crazy about how we ought to walk out. Had a speech and everything like he was just waiting for them to pull something on us. And then they dragged him off and I ain't seen him since."

I thought of the sound the club had made against Grady's skull and how it had hollowed me out.

"What I can't figure," Jess went on, "is how in God's name you missed all that, being that you sniff out trouble like a hound dog."

"I told you I was picking," I said.

"Either stop lying to me, Glo, or shut up," Jess said. Her voice was angry, but there was something broken at the edge, something hurt.

I shut up. And as we turned the corner, I could see the front entrance.

Two more police trucks had pulled up.

And the big heavy gate that had been so easy to walk through was pulled shut and bolted tight.

Something told me St. Peter wouldn't be sitting at his radio the next day, *Dick Tracy* or not.

Suddenly Terrance Bowman wasn't at the top of my list of troubles.

Chapter Twelve

"Stop daydreaming, Gloria, and start picking," Pa said, tossing me my picking sack.

He had just emptied all the peaches I picked into the wheelbarrow below my ladder. That sack had been heavy, cutting across my back and shoulder as I dropped peach after peach after doggone peach into it. It got heavier and heavier like it was trying to hold me down. With every move I made and every step up or down the ladder I went, the weight in the sack shifted and pulled at me. I had to reach out and grab hold of a tree branch once or twice to keep from falling. When Pa finally reached up and took it from me, I was as light as a soap bubble. I could've floated up high in the sky and caught an eastbound wind all the way back to Oklahoma.

But carrying a heavy sack wasn't half as bad as having to look at food all day that I couldn't eat. Earlier when I was stacking peaches in the wheelbarrow, I found one with a big old wormhole in it. It'd gone all soft on one side, with juice dripping out. I figured they were going to throw this one out anyway, I might as well have a bite from the side that wasn't all wormed up. I'd just gotten my teeth in when a man with a clipboard started yelling bloody murder that I was stealing. Then Pa came up and started yelling that I was stealing and making sure the man with the clipboard knew he raised me better than to be a thief. And then I started yelling that I wasn't a thief. I turned that peach around to show them both that it was no good. Man with the clipboard snatched it right out of my hands and said they had a procedure for damaged crop, and it didn't involve a slip like me deciding what was good and what was not. He whistled to someone who brought over a different wheelbarrow that was buzzing with flies and full of rotten fruit, and he tossed my half-good peach right into it. Jess found out later that all they did with the fruit that wouldn't sell was burn it out back.

"They said they didn't want pickers to start

bruising crop on purpose just so they could eat it," she whispered to me.

"I wouldn't bruise nothing on purpose!" I told her. "I don't mind soft fruit. I don't mind if one side is all smashed in. I don't mind if I have to pull a worm out as long as my finger."

"Don't you tell them that," Jess hissed at me.

"Why not? They burning something that could be sitting at the bottom of my belly right now."

"'Cause it'd make them think we're trash," Jess said. "Trash eats trash, and we ain't trash."

And then she went right back to picking like they were paying as much for following dumb rules as they were for peaches, which wasn't much anyway.

"Gloria!" Pa yelled. "What'd I say?"

I slung the empty sack over my shoulder.

"Stop daydreaming and start picking," I said.

"Don't make me say it a third time," said Pa, hoisting the wheelbarrow up and walking off towards the sorting house.

"He's barking at me like I'm one of his hired hands," I grumbled.

"You *are* a hired hand, Gloria," spouted Jess, who was picking on the other side of the tree. "And right now, you ain't pulling your weight."

I snapped a peach off a branch. Usually I liked working with Pa. Back in Oklahoma he was stern enough, but now, he was chiding me and acting like I was an embarrassment or something. Or he was afraid I'd get him in trouble. Or he was just afraid. And normally I would have talked his ear off about baseball and me showing a group of boys I was made of stronger stuff than they thought.

But I didn't want to tell him. Not just because I'd ducked work. But because it felt good to keep something from him. It felt good to know something he didn't. To know something Jess didn't. To know something Ma didn't.

Just then I saw Quentin's mop of hair pass under me. He sure was clean and polished as a whistle, but his hair was made of more wayward stuff.

"Psst!" I whispered so Jess couldn't hear. She was halfway up another tree anyway.

Quentin looked up. "Gloria!" he whispered back. There might have been a whole tree of peaches between us, but I could swear there was a smile on Quentin's face.

"What's happening?" I asked. "With the team?"

Quentin shook his head. "Laying low. Can't get out. Gate is shut tight, and there are four men standing by. If you ask me, boss is spooked."

"Well, there's gotta be another way."

Quentin blinked. "Nothing we can do. They got curfew, and they got coppers. More than last time."

"Last time?"

"When they took Jimmy's pa."

"Oh . . . Well, ain't there any way else out?"

Quentin shook his head. "Took us a while to figure out how to time sneaking out in the first place. We're supposed to play the apricot boys on Sunday, but I don't know how we could."

"All right, so make a new plan! Who figured out the *Dick Tracy* thing? Was it you?"

Quentin smiled and looked like I'd just handed him a ham sandwich with pickles. He nodded once and stuck his hands in his pockets almost like he was embarrassed he'd thought of something so smart.

"All right then, so we need a *new* plan!"

The word "we" had tumbled out of my mouth.

The sunniness on Quentin's face shaded over. "Listen, Gloria, I don't know how to bust out of here. If I knew, I'd tell you. But the fact is, it's Terrance's team, not mine. If you're to have any part of it, busting out or playing the apricots, Terrance needs to say so."

"Why you let him have his way on everything?"

"Truth is, Gloria, everyone I know here I know because of Terrance. It was Terrance who got us together. Well, him and Jimmy. Means something, you know?"

I yanked another peach off and tossed it in my

bag. "Well, I don't wanna have to talk to that no-good lying son of a gun ever again."

"Well," said Quentin. "You might not have to. Don't think there's enough time to break out anyways. Not all that many peaches left."

He was right. How many Sundays did they have left to play the apricot boys? One? Maybe two?

"Say, you're from Balko, right?" he asked.

"Yep."

A glimmer went up in his eyes. "I was thinking that rings a bell . . ."

"Anyone else here from there?" I asked.

"Not sure . . . but if there is, I'll be the one to find out. Say, maybe you know my cousin—"

"Move on, son," said a man with a clipboard, and Quentin darted away.

"Nuts," I whispered, and rubbed my eyes. Whatever it was they sprayed on the crop made your nose red and raw and your eyes itch.

"California, you are a bust," I said for the thousandth time that day.

"Maybe it wouldn't be such a *bust* if you spent more time making the most of it and less time complaining," said Jess, who was coming up the ladder across from me and rubbing at her own eyes.

I pulled myself up another rung. "You *like* it here?"

Jess didn't say anything but I could hear her rustling in the tree.

"It ain't about what I like or don't like, Gloria," she said. "Sometimes you gotta just . . ."

She trailed off and the branches rustled a bit more.

"What?" I asked.

"Nothing."

It wasn't nothing. She was holding her tongue when she wanted to wag it.

I snapped a dead, shriveled-up peach off a branch, aimed just to the left of Jess's ear, and sent the dead thing whizzing at her. She sensed it coming and her arms went flying around her face.

"Sometimes you just gotta *what*?"

"*Grow up*, Gloria, sometimes you just gotta *grow up!*"

And with that she bounded down her ladder to empty her sack below me.

"I ain't no baby!" I hollered down at her.

"You acting like one!" she hollered back.

"At least I ain't bossing nobody around! You like a doggone stone in my shoe."

She was stacking peaches furiously below. "You think I *like* bossing you? I don't. Lord, what I'd give to have no one to mind but myself."

"So mind yourself! No one's forcing you to be a nag."

She threw her head back to look up at me. "First off, Gloria, *I* ain't a nag. *You* a pill. Secondly, in case you haven't noticed, Ma and Pa on me all the time to mind you. It's 'Make sure Gloria does this,' 'Make sure Gloria don't do that.' You wearing them out, and you wearing me out."

Between the itching in my eyes and Jess nosing me every which way, I'd had about as much as I could take. I broke a twig off the tree, green leaves and all. "Soon as I save up enough wages," I said, "you won't have to worry about me. I'll shove off, and you can get back to doing whatever it is you do when you don't have to mind me."

Jess climbed back up the ladder. "Oh, you saving your wages? Gloria, your wages going straight to the truck so we can move on. Your wages going straight to electricity and rent and the company store for that matter. Shoot, Gloria, your wages already spoken for."

She was right. We were still having tiny fritters in the morning and now corn mush washed down with salt-and-pepper tea in the evening. They wouldn't let Ma leave to go to the town grocer unless she was leaving for good. So it was all company store food from now on, and none of it was paid for yet. Pa was still barking orders, Ma was still acting like things weren't as bad as they were, and I still wasn't playing baseball.

And it wasn't just the fact that there was no way

out. Terrance had made a deal with me and then tried to go back on his word. I would've struck Clyde out, I knew I would have. But something told me even if we could play baseball, Terrance would lock me out of the team on a technicality. He'd done it on purpose. Even if he hadn't known the coppers were coming, he'd tried to throw me off and make the other boys see me as a burden. He'd tried to turn them against me, poison the well, so to speak. I yanked another dead branch off the tree just to hear it snap.

Maybe it wasn't so bad. The boys wanted me in, I knew they did. Maybe I could somehow get the clipboard men to let us play after picking in the area right outside the gate to the orchard. Maybe I could start my own team somehow. Maybe I could—

A thin, piercing wail sounded from below. I looked down and saw that lady with the faded pink dress and the little baby coming our way. Behind her was her man, tall with the high cheekbones, empty-eyed and paying no mind to the little howl he was following. The girl had slung the baby over her hip, and he was crying up into the sky. Out of the corner of my eye I saw Jess get real still. The girl bounced the baby on her hip once or twice to calm him down, but all it did was jostle his cry and make him throw his head back like a rag doll.

"Don't stare, Gloria," Jess whispered through

the leaves, even though she was looking herself.

I reached up and found a peach with my left hand. The wail got higher, more raw. I could see the baby's pinched little red face, I could see his hands shuddering. The girl slid out of the sling and set the baby on his back so she could climb up and pick while he was lying there alone.

His hollering went wild and awful once he was on the ground. It flooded my ears and made my own throat go raw, like I was the one yelling my head off. I figured she was going up for just a moment. And then I realized she was going to stay up in the tree until she filled her whole sack, baby crying and all.

"That ain't right," I whispered to Jess. "She oughtta pick that baby up."

Jess was still looking at the baby, her hands moving slowly around the branches. "She trying to keep the itchy stuff outta his eyes," she said quietly. "Best she leave him on the ground."

"I don't like hearing him cry," I said.

"I know," Jess whispered.

I climbed up higher into the tree, but that baby was crying out loud. He didn't know how to shut up or keep on keeping on. He just wailed and wailed.

I went all the way to the top rung, ladder groaning and creaking under me. I felt it buckle and held on to the tree branch hard.

"Don't you mind it, Glo," Jess said softly. "Don't you pay it no mind . . ."

But the scream was filling up my ears with awful. It had been a while since I heard a cry like that, and I didn't like thinking about the last time. I didn't want to look, but I looked anyway, and I saw the little thing wriggling on the ground, trying with all his might to push against the ratty old quilt he was wrapped in. His fingers splayed out like he was looking for a braid or a collar to hold on to.

If that were Ma's baby, she would have picked him up. She would have picked him up and cooed and sang and bounced him until he quieted. She would have held him long after he got quiet and then laid him down. She wouldn't have let him think he was alone for a second.

"I gotta get out of this tree, Jess," I said. "Take my peaches to the sorting house, will you?"

I didn't give her enough time to reply. I shot down the ladder and dropped my picking sack next to the wheelbarrow.

"Hey, you!" called one of the clipboard men. "You bruising product!"

But I kept walking. That little yowl was bigger than the whole orchard, and if I didn't get out of earshot, I didn't know what I was going to do.

Just as I burst through the trees, the long howl

of the evening alarm sounded. But even though I walked hard and fast, I couldn't stop thinking about that little kid crying out. And worse, I couldn't stop thinking about Little Si and how he sounded when he couldn't breathe.

When I got to 72 it looked sadder and sorrier that I remembered. It looked like disappointment. It looked like not having enough. Worse, it looked like giving up. I caught a glimpse of Ma through the window. Probably cooking up mush or fritters or something else there wouldn't be enough of.

I couldn't bear the thought of being alone with her, even for a few minutes. I couldn't bear the way she tried to smile through the measly dinners and I sure as heck couldn't look her in the eye with that baby's cry still ricocheting around in my brain. It was easier to be around her with Pa or Jess there, but when it was just me and her, I wanted to slip through the cracks in the floor. I'd rather get a scolding from Pa for being late for dinner than have to sit with Ma in the suffocating dark.

I took off running. Past rows of boxy shanties, past ropes of clotheslines, past skinny kids hanging out of windows. I raced past a sea of tired eyes and tired arms pulling little kids along home. I raced past men tinkering on their trucks and barefoot kids shooting marbles. I barreled straight into a woman with her arms full of cans, nearly sending them rolling into the dust.

"Watch where you're going!" she shouted after me, but I was already turning the corner, trying to find some bit of calm, some bit of blue sky, some bit of wide open, even if it was on the other side of chain link fence.

Finally, I reached the edge of the camp, breathing hard. And in front of me, beyond the tall chain link, was green and blue and wind and sky. I hooked my fingers through metal. If I could climb that fence, if I could somehow get over the barbed wire, I could run and run. Not in straight rows, but in zigzags and spirals, over stones and over creeks. Through dark evergreen bushes and soft brown pine needles. Under trees that grew different shapes and heights. Under a sky that stretched and soared.

If I concentrated hard enough, I could tune out the sounds of the camp behind me. If I closed my eyes, I could hear the birds and shutterbugs, the rushing of the breeze in the trees, the sweet sound of a creek nearby. Probably the same creek that ran past wherever it was Terrance and the boys played. If I closed my eyes, I was almost somewhere else. I was almost standing in a wide-open field staring down a batter with a baseball in my hand.

I threw my back against the fence and sank

down. Looking up, I caught the white glint of the barbed wire that curled around and around the top. Something about all that fence around all that land just felt wrong. Wrong or not, there was no way over.

I pushed back against the chain link and pressed my chin into my knees. Over in the orchard, a few sorry-looking trees swayed gently in the breeze with a handful of rotting peaches slowly sinking into the dirt below.

But there was something else. Something in the fence. I squinted. All those tiny chain link diamonds warped and curved in one spot. I looked closer. Someone or something had bent the chain link up. It wasn't much—it was just high enough to slip an arm, and maybe a shoulder under.

I couldn't go *over*. But it sure looked like with a little pulling and a little digging, I might just be able to go *under*.

And maybe, just maybe, I could get more than one of us out.

Maybe I could break a whole baseball team out of this joint.

Even if I did need Terrance Bowman to let me do it.

Chapter Thirteen

The morning alarm had just sounded and I bounded out the door ahead of Ma, Pa, and Jess.

"Where you running to? I know you ain't trying to get picking faster!" called Jess.

"Maybe I *am*!" I shouted, and ran ahead.

I darted in and out of the gathering crowd. Everyone was stomping towards work and talking up a storm. There was chatter—some of it hushed and low, some of it biting and angry. Cutting wages was more than a rumor now. Some people were saying it was going down by one cent an hour and wouldn't be so bad, and others were claiming they were cutting it by a whole nickel and *someone ought to do something about it.* I didn't give a fig being that my wages weren't even my wages, and Ma and Pa had all but told us to keep our heads down.

I had more important things to worry about anyway.

I needed to find Terrance before the orchard swallowed us up into different corners. I was just about to start hollering his name when I saw the back of his cap tilted just off to the side. I ran to catch up with him until I was at his shoulder.

"Terrance Bowman!"

He kept his gaze fixed ahead. "I ain't got nothing to say to you."

"Bet you will when you hear what it is I got to tell."

The crowd was slowing and gathering at the main gate to the orchard. Up ahead I could see that same man with the plum-colored silk on his hat standing on that same makeshift platform. It looked like he was going to make another speech.

"Quiet down! Quiet down now!" the man called out, but the crowd was humming like an old engine that wouldn't quit.

"Listen, Terrance," I said, "I don't like you, and it's clear as day you don't much like me, neither. Shoot, first you go saying I ain't got the disposition to play and next thing you're going back on a deal we spat and shook on. How 'bout we call it even, huh?"

"How 'bout you shove off?"

"Quiet now!" the man yelled over the crowd.

"You know, Terrance, I might. But then I got to thinking. You and me, we got *common interests*. I want to play baseball and—"

"And I got a baseball team. Don't mean there's room for you on it, no matter what your pitch is like."

"You may have a team, but you ain't got no place to play now that curfew's on, the camp's locked, and they got folks patrolling the grounds."

"Order! I say order!" said the man with the hat, but the crowd was getting louder.

"What's it to you?" Terrance said, raising his voice to be heard.

"I want in."

"Fat chance."

"I think there's a good chance."

"How you figure that?"

"I know how to get out."

Terrance slowly turned to face me and unfolded his arms from across his chest. The crowd was restless and rippling, but he was as still as a high-summer pond.

"Go on," he said.

I smiled. "You think I'm just gonna tell you what I know?"

"Nope. I expect you gonna ask something in return."

"You expect right."

The man in the hat was shouting *"Order!"* but the crowd was still flapping their mouths, and Terrance and I were still flapping ours.

"I want on the team," I said. "I wanna play."

Terrance rolled his head back like he'd had just about enough of me. "If you think *for one minute* I'm gonna let some mousy little bag of hot air like you set conditions for *my team*, then you got a—"

A hush ripped through the crowd and dried up all the talking around us. It was like someone had flicked a switch. Everyone was looking at something, and I stood on my tiptoes to get a peek.

The man with the plum-colored silk was still standing on the platform. But now he wasn't alone. On either side of him were about a dozen police officers, billy clubs in hand, just like the one that had struck the back of Grady's head. Next to me, Terrance tensed up and cursed under his breath.

"There now," the man in the hat said. He was looking more sure of himself now that he had company. "Now, I don't control the price of crops, I wish to heaven I did. The price of peaches is what it is, and

wages are what they are. You want something different, you can go on your way, it's a free country and I
won't stop you. But anyone here talking Red is going
to get personally escorted out by these gentlemen."

The policemen were stock-still, a sea of deep blue
against the white suit of the man with the hat.

"There's a million folks I could find right now
who'd be happy to finish bringing this crop in.
Heck, I could find a million more willing to work for
half of what I'm paying you. I'm giving you a chance
to walk away right now. You want to stay and work,
you stay and work for sixteen cents an hour—"

A thousand breaths exploded into the air like the
whole crowd got punched in the stomach at once.

"We hire hardworking Americans with guts and
grit. We don't hire folks who want something for
nothing. We don't hire *degenerates*. So listen up.
After eight p.m., anyone found outside the gates will
be *personally escorted off the property.*"

I looked over at Terrance. His jaw was clenched
tight, and his eyes were flaming wild.

"Anyone congregating in groups at any time of
day will be *personally escorted off the property.* We
employ good, decent folks here, not lazy sons of
guns, not rabble-rousers, not Reds. And might I
remind you, we are not afraid to get rough with any
lowlife causing trouble."

Terrance hissed another curse under his breath.

"And anyone caught distributing contraband materials, leaflets, and pamphlets will be *personally escorted off the property*. Have I made myself clear?"

No one answered.

"Good," said the man in the white hat. "Now, anyone who has a problem with any of these terms, I invite you to pack your bags and leave. Otherwise, get to work."

In front of us, two clipboard men unlocked the gates to the orchard and swung them open wide with a lonely metal creak. The crowd shuffled forwards, pushing me along with them. I'd just about figured there was no point in pressing Terrance any further when he caught me suddenly by the elbow and pulled me off to the side.

"Now listen up," he said, his eyes looking harder and older than I remembered. "I've had about enough of fences, and I'm sick of curfews. Sick of people watching me like a hawk, telling me where I can and can't go. So you know what? You got a deal. You bust me out of this place where I don't got no one breathing down my neck, you can play. *Forget* about pitching, though."

And then he let go and rejoined the group.

Figured.

"Terrance!" I called.

He turned.

"How am I gonna—I mean what are we—what's the plan?"

In two paces, he was back in my face. "Quentin'll set it up. The meeting. It'll have to be after dark."

A cool breeze wrapped around my ears.

"Or are you scared of getting *personally escorted off the property?*"

I knew well enough to shake my head. But I felt a thumping in my ribs and a tingling in my fingertips that hadn't been there before. I watched Terrance disappear into a sea of faded blue jeans and thin skirts flapping in the breeze like he'd broken a thousand curfews before.

"Who's that?"

I spun around to see Jess with a look like she'd sucked down lemons.

"No one," I said, and slipped back into the crowd.

Sunlight beat down on the top of my head, making my scalp burn. I was as high as I could get on a ladder, the earth miles below me, far enough to make some folks queasy.

I wasn't queasy, but I sure felt skittish waiting for word on the plan. Suppose there was none? Suppose the team was working on their own way out? Or worse, suppose they'd found the secret spot at the edge of camp? Worse still, suppose a clipboard man had seen it and was already sealing it off?

I heard the sound of a groaning ladder across from me and saw that someone was climbing up the other side of the trunk. I figured I better look busy, so I started picking as fast as I could.

"Psst, Gloria!"

It was Quentin peeping through the leaves with a finger to his lips. I could have jumped and shouted hallelujah, I was so happy to see him.

"Terrance says you found an alternate point of egress. Is it true?"

"Alternate point of egress?"

"Another way out."

I beamed. "Sure is."

Quentin was about as cool and collected as they come, but even I could see the smile dancing at the edges of his mouth.

"Well, all right. Listen up. We meet at ten tonight when the shift at the front gate changes."

"I don't got a pocket watch, Quentin—"

"Don't worry. The guard that takes off at ten has got a car that sounds like a tommy gun when he starts it up. You hear that, you slip out quiet and quick. Anyone who sees you, you tell them you got to go to the john. Just be inconspicuous."

"Inconspicuous?"

"Try not to get caught."

"Got it," I said.

"We meet in Old Man Grady's cabin. It's still empty," Quentin said. "When you come, you tap 'shave and a haircut' on the door. We'll let you in."

"Sure thing, boss."

Quentin smiled, and I could almost see the rosy blush coming through the leaves. "Me? I'm not the boss. That's Terrance."

"Say, how come Terrance so bullish? What's he got to prove anyway? Is it true he got a ma on the run and his pa's on the bottle?"

Quentin's clear eyes darted back to mine and I suddenly wanted to shrink behind the leaves for talking that way about Terrance's folks. I wasn't even sure why I said it. The summer sun started burning up in my cheeks, and for a moment, I was worried that Quentin might get the wrong idea about me. That all I had in me was spite. But he just plucked a peach and looked it over like I'd asked the most earnest, fair question in the world.

"I couldn't say exactly why Terrance is the way he is," Quentin said. "He doesn't talk much about all that . . . but I expect it's on his mind all the time. . . . Might be hard to tell sometimes, but deep down inside, Terrance Bowman's as good as gold."

I liked how Quentin talked, cool and calm and easy. He didn't have an ounce of meanness in him, and I wondered how he could come all the way from Oklahoma on the same roads I did, be stuck in the same dingy kind of shanty as me, be picking peaches and rubbing spray out of his eyes like me, and still be as kind and thoughtful as he was. I guessed he was just cut from a different cloth.

"I better go," he said.

"All right then, I'll see you tonight."

He smiled one last time and ducked down out of sight. I got to picking again, and then I heard his voice calling—

"Hey, Gloria!"

"Yeah?" I called back.

"I remember who it is that's from Balko around here."

I almost jumped the fifteen feet down from the top of the tree. "Who?"

"One of the apricot kids. Not on the team, but he's come to a game or two."

"What's his name?"

"Ben Franklin. But he says most people know him as Joe Franklin's son."

Chapter Fourteen

If I hadn't been waiting for a secret meeting, I would've been as tired and done with the day as Ma and Pa. They were wound up extra tight, whispering and shooting their eyes my way to make sure I wasn't listening. But I didn't need their lousy secrets. I had my own. And by the end of the night, I'd be on a real team, even if I wasn't pitcher. When Pa said it was time for bed, I just nodded and crawled under the covers and shut my eyes tight.

It didn't take long for Jess to be out cold, but I didn't let myself sleep. I had the buzz of planning and knowing things racing through my veins, and not the day's sun or the hours of climbing, or the empty, howling space in my gut, could pull me under. Pretty soon I could hear Pa's gentle snore and Ma's deep breaths. Ma had a funny way of breathing when she slept. Like she was holding her breath all day so that at night her lungs had to drink extra deep to get her going again in the morning.

And then I heard it.

Sput-sput-RA-TAT-TAT-TAT-TAT-TAT-TAT!

It was the tommy-gun car that Quentin had talked about, had to be. They were changing shifts at the gate. I sat up slow and silent and carefully pulled the sheet back. The air was blowing ice chills and my legs went all gooseflesh.

Better get my overalls.

I listened hard to Ma and Pa while keeping my eyes locked on Jess. Her hand was up by her face, uncurled and resting easy. One strap of my overalls went over my shoulder. Then the other one. I slipped my boots on and laced them tight. Last thing I needed was to be tripping over myself while trying to be inconspicuous.

I slunk out the front door, knitting my ribs together and praying I didn't get butterfingers and let it slip and slam closed. But I was careful and it didn't and just like that I was out in the night air. Me and the night birds and the mischief-makers.

The rows of cabins were dark and tired-looking.

There wasn't a soul moving about. I was careful to sneak through the darkest areas and sidestepped the rings of floodlights like they were puddles. Now and then a rustle would catch my ear, but I kept my head down and kept on going.

Grady's cabin was the last one on the row. It had a cemetery silence around it. Could be this was all some trick to get me licked. Could be St. Peter himself was waiting in there. Terrance didn't want me on the team, that much was clear. I just wondered if he was the sorry sort to set me up and turn me in.

I tapped "shave and a haircut, two bits" on the door like Quentin said and stood there waiting. All I could hear was a steady trill of night bugs, the song tight and long in the air.

But then there was a rustle behind the door, a flurry of whispers, and it cracked open just enough for me to see the white of Quentin's eye.

"It's her," he whispered, and then he whipped open the door and pulled me in quick.

It was endlessly black inside. I could hear the boys fidgeting. As my eyes got accustomed to the dark, their faces appeared, one by one. There was no laughing, no taunting, not even a smirk. They were looking at me and holding their breath.

"Well," said Terrance after a moment. "We all here. Whatchu got."

I swallowed. My mouth was made of sand and grit. "You told them my terms?"

Terrance nodded.

I looked down at the toes of my boots. Then I looked up and took a breath and started talking. "The front gate's locked. No leaving that way, not with them watching, and there's more of them watching now."

Some of the boys nodded.

"And we fenced in all around. I expect y'all are good climbers, but that barbed wire would cut you to shreds."

More nodding. And a few "mm-hmms."

"But," I said, "I found a spot we can get out—"

"Hold up, Gloria," Quentin said.

He scrambled forward with a stick of chalk in his hand. In the dark blue evening light, he started to draw something on the floor of Grady's cabin. We sat silently watching him. He was drawing a map of the orchard on the floor. He drew in perfect straight lines that glowed dimly in the dark. And then, careful not to smear his drawing, he leaned over and handed me the chalk.

Quentin's map of camp was perfect. There was the main front gate with St. Peter's little booth. There was the wide expanse of the orchard, marked with little circles for trees, the sorting house, and the cannery where Ma worked most of the time, the fence that separated the shanties from the trees with the wide gate marked with two little notches. There were the shanties, row after row of them. I didn't have to ask to know that Quentin had marked the exact number of lines for the exact number of rows. He'd memorized the layout of the camp perfectly. During the day, I felt like the place could swallow me up whole. And now here it was, at my fingertips.

"This is us," Quentin said, gently tapping a small *x* he'd marked over one of the shanty lines for Grady's place. "Where can we get out?"

I heard the sounds of knees shuffling closer and felt the space close up around me. Slowly, I reached my arm across the chalk map, finding the place with the bend in the fence with my eyes.

I turned the chalk over in my hand. With one stroke I could show them all the way out, earn my place on the team, and be on my way to playing baseball instead of picking peaches. With one stroke, I could show them all I was worth something, that I could keep secrets and I could make secrets. That was all it would take. But I couldn't do it, not without making one more play.

"Wait—" I said.

All sixteen eyes shot up.

"Terrance," I said, "you told them you'd let me play if I showed y'all a way out?"

Terrance nodded, a gash of moonlight across his face.

I rolled the chalk between my fingers. "What position?"

Terrance looked peeved. "Something between outfield and pitching, ain't that what you—"

"I wanna pitch."

"I'm the pitcher, ain't up for debating."

"I wanna pitch."

"We already got that taken care of—"

"I wanna pitch or no deal."

The air between Terrance and me pulled tight and taut. And even though my eyes were locked into his, I could feel the gaze of every other boy whip around us. Everyone was leaned in close, hope whispering silently up to the ceiling. Hope that we'd get out, hope we'd beat the Michelson's boys . . . hope Terrance would pick up what I was putting down.

"Terrance," Casey said after a moment. "It ain't a *bad* idea . . ."

"She's good," Clyde chimed in. "She's . . . uh . . . she's pretty good."

Terrance's face was tightly drawn, like he was struggling to hold it still. He was cornered whether he said yes or no. I could see it in his eyes. The boys wanted to play. He could give me and them what we wanted at the same time . . . or spend however many Sundays were left slinging peaches into his sack and rubbing spray out of his eyes.

"Deal," Terrance said softly, eyes on the ground.

The word was faint, but it was there, he'd said it. But it was too easy, too fast.

"Swear it," I said.

He rolled his eyes. "I swear."

"No, swear it on *something*."

He got up on his knees. "I swear on all that's holy—"

"Everyone swears on that."

"I swear on my honor—"

"I don't believe you."

"I swear on all the peaches in California—"

"Now you're just playing with me."

He swallowed hard and leaned across the chalk map as far as he could. His eyes were steely and dark against the flecks of moonlight that painted the cabin floor and spilled across the boys' faces.

"I swear on my mother, you show us a way out, you can play and you can pitch."

Every pair of eyes, which had been fixed on me, turned slowly to look at Terrance. He looked tired, defeated, like bringing her up had knocked the wind out of him. I knew better than to ask for something else. I nodded my head once and held out my hand. Terrance took it and we shook with an icy calm between us that I knew wouldn't last forever.

But something had sparked on in me. The thousands of nos I'd heard from the Balko boys, every time a door had shut in my face, every time someone had told me to hush up, it all came clattering down around me in that tiny little cabin. The world was suddenly wide and broad and full. I took a sip of the sweet, sweet air and started talking.

"So like I said, whole camp is locked up tight. They got curfew going, they telling us not to meet, telling us no contraband materials."

Clyde was nodding and nodding. Casey was bouncing his leg. I'd never done anything like this before, but suddenly I felt I'd waited my whole life to give a speech. "Far as I know, baseball ain't contraband, not yet anyway!"

There was head-nodding and a growing murmur that bordered on dangerous for a supposedly secret meeting. But I just let it fill me up, and I kept going.

"Far as I know, there's no law against organizing a team! Ain't that right?"

The murmurs burst into cheers of "Yes!"

Quentin raised a hand for quiet, and the group reined in their hollering. I set my voice to a low whisper.

"So listen up. What we need is an *alternate point of egress*! There's a bend in the fence here," I said, marking the spot with another *x*. "You can see it 'cause the chain link makes a ripple—looks like a trick on the eye. It's bent *up*, see? Just past the fence there's a whole bunch of bushes, and beyond that, a creek. You get beyond the fence, you duck right into those bushes, and you out.

"So here's the plan, tomorrow during picking hours, you make it a point of excusing yourself to head to the john often as possible. You make sure no one's looking at you, and then, you dig. One of y'all got a spade or something?"

A handful of arms went up.

"All right then. We do this right, we can get her done in a few days and make it to Sunday's game. Whaddya say?"

It was quiet, but all the ice chill between me and Terrance had gone out of the air and a summer warmth spread throughout Grady's empty cabin. And then all at once, the boys surrounded me and were asking questions, where I was from, where I'd picked before, where I'd learned to pitch. The questions kept coming, one right after the other so that I could only half answer one before someone asked something else. Names were coming at me from every angle.

"I'm Rudy! I'll bring the spade!"

"Eugene here! I'm second baseman!"

"Holden! And I was rooting for you from the start!"

I felt like I'd eaten a ham dinner with all the fixings, like the wind was at my back and a dollar was sitting in my pocket.

"All right, all right." Terrance's voice cut through. "Let's wrap it up."

Everyone quieted, and even though Terrance had interrupted what was going on, my face was full of smile. The air was thick with hope and bursting with unsung cheers and hollers.

"Let's get on home now," he said. "One at a time. Ain't nobody gonna believe us if we say all nine of us had to take a leak at the same time. Everybody clear on what needs doing?"

There was a whisper-chorus of agreement, and Quentin peeked through the window to make sure the coast was clear. One by one, each boy disappeared into the night until it was just me, Terrance, and Quentin.

Terrance and I met eyes for a second. "You got what you want," he said. "You best not let us down."

A bit of danger crept into the air. He'd be watching me. Making sure I was true to my word, that I wasn't full of hot air. I wasn't. If he was hoping I'd blow their cover, or I was afraid of getting caught, or that my arm would somehow go weak and floppy before Sunday, he was wrong.

Terrance was tougher than all the Balko boys put together, but I'd fought my way onto his team and into his position, tooth and nail. I felt like cartwheeling, even in the small space of Grady's cabin.

"All right, Gloria, you're next, wait till I say go," said Quentin.

"Nah," I said. "You go on ahead. I owe ya."

Quentin beamed in the dark. "Count to fifty and then go. And don't get caught," he said.

"I won't."

He tipped his cap and went out, silent as a cat.

I stood still, counting softly like Quentin told me to. The feeling of being alone and the idea of getting caught made me want to race through those numbers and get back as quick as possible. But I went even and slow, like I was walking a tightrope.

"Fifty."

I pulled my cap down low around my ears and reached for the door. And just then the tip of my boot caught on something and I stumbled.

"Son of a gun!" I said, turning around to see what I'd tripped on.

It was one of the floorboards, sticking up just enough to give me trouble. I knelt down to push it back into place, but it gave way easily beneath my hands. Someone had pried the whole plank up. I pulled it back and peered into the hollow space below the boards.

"Son of a gun . . ."

Below the floorboard were two stacks of little pamphlets tied neatly with string. On the cover was a picture of a man in a cap and overalls looking towards a rising sun. Behind him was a family, three children and a woman with her hand on the man's shoulders. All around them read the words:

Fair Wages Are Worth Striking For!

Join your fellow worker for COMMON DECENCY and COMMON GOALS and COMMON GOOD!

I didn't know exactly what the leaflets were for, but I knew that anything someone hid under the floorboards was something you didn't want to get caught looking at. Especially not here. *Especially* not after meeting in a group after curfew.

Still, I picked one stack up, then the other, and ran my thumb along the sides. The paper was thin . . . there must have been a couple hundred leaves there, a little crinkly from getting damp and then dry again. I turned them over in my hand. On the back, written in pencil, was the name *Michelson's.*

The apricot orchard.

The air was sparking again. I placed the floorboard

back over the opening but held on to the papers. I'd already broken two of the new camp rules with the meeting in a group and then being out after eight.

Might as well break a third.

I shoved the smaller stack of leaflets into my pocket, put the rest back under the floorboards, and set out into the night.

Heading back to 72, I was alive! I was breathing in all the humming of the earth, all its liveliness in the singing bugs, the flickering stars, and the thrum-hush of the peach trees bending in the wind! Each sip of air was sugar syrup, and with each step the whole earth slung me back up into the night. I was part of a secret plan. I was part of a secret plan to escape to go win a baseball game, I was going to strike out Arlon Mackie, and if that wasn't exciting enough, I had *contraband material* in my pocket!

And 72 wasn't a dead dark place but my place, that old truck wasn't some busted-up jalopy, it was my truck, and in the cabin was my baseball, come all the way from a field in Texas. I pushed the door inward, gentle like a little baby was sleeping on the other side. Pa was snoring and Ma was breathing deep and Jessamyn was as still as a maiden in a fairy tale.

I shivered down under the covers next to her,

but just when I was about to get settled, her eyes snapped open.

"Gloria Mae," she whispered calmly, "I don't know what you're up to, but you better let me in on it if you don't want Ma or Pa to hear every detail of how you snuck out and just how long you were gone. So spill it, sister."

Part Three

Chapter Fifteen

"Jess!" I called, pulling an ugly little peach from the top of one of the trees. I'd been tossing her peaches all morning and she'd been catching them, even though we both knew being caught flinging the crop around was like getting caught playing with matches in a hayloft. I found her eyes through the leaves and grinned.

When I told Jess about the game and the boys, she didn't fly up and tattle on me. She listened in the dark. When I was done, she lay back down. And so did I. I stared at the low ceiling for a bit until she said, "So you got leaflets talking wages and walkout in your pocket?"

I shifted onto my side. "Um . . . yes . . ."

"All of 'em?"

"Um . . . no . . ."

"Give 'em here."

I handed them over and prepared to be personally escorted out of camp. After a while she said, "So you think things are as bad over at the apricot orchard as they are here?"

"I dunno, but I guess Grady thought they were."

"And what exactly were you thinking bringing something like this back here?"

I fumbled a few words in the dark, but nothing came out right. I could hear her thumbing the edges of leaflets like a flip book. It made a purring sound, like a cat.

"Hmmm," said Jess.

"Oh, Jess . . ."

"Yeah, Gloria?"

"I got it on good authority that Joe Franklin's sweet son is just down the road, picking apricots."

The purring sound stopped.

"Hmm," Jess said. We both lay there and then she sat up in bed. I was almost sure she was about to turn me in when I heard the tin pop of Jess's coffee can that had all her starlet cutouts in it.

"You can't just have contraband on your person, Glo. You and I both know these would be flying out of your pocket left and right if you keep 'em on you."

That was true. She was probably going to tell me to put them back, or burn them, or turn them in and have the clipboard men rip apart the rest of Grady's cabin looking for who-knows-what.

"I think I'll keep them here," she said, fastening the tin top back on in the dark. She lay back down again, making the thin sheet that divided the room flutter just a little.

"So let me get this right," she said. "You gonna dig under the fence with a garden spade?"

It hadn't sounded stupid until it came out of her mouth.

"Um . . . yeah . . . ," I answered in the dark.

"Hmmm," she said.

"You gonna tell Ma and Pa?"

She turned over on her side and beat her thin little pillow with her fist. "Well, that depends," she answered.

"Depends on what?"

She let my question hang in the air like cigarette smoke, curling and filling the whole room up with itself.

"On whether or not you let me in on it."

I rubbed my feet together under the covers.

"You wanna play baseball?" I asked. This would

be the end of me. I might be on the team now, but it was still a democracy. Telling them they had to take my sister, who couldn't throw and couldn't hit, would get me voted out in an instant.

"No. I just . . . want somewhere else to be."

I didn't have to ask to know where.

"Those boys are gonna hold my feet to the fire for this."

"Nah," Jess said. "Not when they see what I can do with a spade."

I felt her grin without seeing it.

The next day it was Jess who began the digging, and Jess who knew that water could do more to loosen up the soil than a spade could. It was Jess who bent down and carefully wedged the spade between the wires of the fence to loosen them a little more and Jess who carried dirt in her pockets and sifted it through her fingers like she was checking for wind and rain.

After she'd done what she could without getting caught, she'd walked right up to Terrance. I watched them from between the tree leaves, praying that my luck would hold, half expecting him to come find me and tell me I'd blown it. But he just nodded. Because Jess knew something none of us did, which is that men in white suits with clipboards get real polite and nervous around a girl in a skirt moaning that she needs to use the john.

"Lady troubles," she'd sigh, and the men would part for her like she was Moses standing at the Red Sea.

After two days, me and a couple other of the smaller boys could wriggle through, but that wouldn't work for Clyde, whose shoulders were wider than Pa's. So we kept digging. All of us. But the truth was, no one worked harder than Terrance. Even when it wasn't his turn, he'd volunteer to go, though it meant he might get caught. I couldn't help but think he was trying to prove himself after getting beat. As long as it got us out sooner, I didn't care what he did.

We kept practicing, too. Each time one of the boys passed me, he'd throw me something. Sometimes stones, which I caught with my right hand till I felt bold enough to catch them with my left, even all the way up in the trees. Sometimes peach pits, left from some stolen piece of fruit, flying light and needing to be caught gently so they wouldn't bounce out of your hand. They threw me heavier stones they pried out of the ground with two hands, which made the tree branches sway when I caught them. Between the throwing and the catching and the climbing, I could feel my right arm getting thicker and stronger. Would've gotten even bigger if I'd had eggs to go with the sorry little pan fritters. Only Terrance kept his distance, though sometimes I'd see him flinging a stone across the fence.

But we weren't the only ones buzzing. As we dug, others were humming, too. The police outside the gate grew in numbers, especially after leaflets reading *Fair Wages Are Worth Striking For!* popped up overnight like mushrooms. I figured there had to be someone else that knew about them because little stacks of them started appearing in every nook and cranny at camp. They were in the cannery, slipped between boxes, and in the sorting house at the bottom of wheelbarrows. They were tucked on the other side of the door to the johns and even hanging on clotheslines. I was smiling about it till five grown men got booted out for uttering the word "strike" under their breath when a clipboard man was close enough to hear.

At least there was no head-splitting that I could see. But when Pa watched them go, even though the clipboard men kept saying not to look and to keep on working, he looked like he had about as much scheming and planning in him as me.

"See, Gloria?" Clyde whispered to me one day. "They got the front gate locked 'cause they cut wages over with the apricot orchard, too. They figure if we get talking to one another the whole place is gonna go Red!"

Suddenly people were more excited about that

word than they'd been when we were waiting in the bushes. I smiled because those clipboard men had no idea that we were closer to talking to the apricot boys than any of our mas and pas were. Except we weren't interested in talking about wages. Just beating them fair and square. At baseball.

The ugly peach landing in Jess's hand made a satisfying *thud*. She grinned up at me as she caught it, as if to say *See, I can do it, too!* But it wasn't mocking, or teasing, or trying to get me riled up. It was like a wink. Like we were both part of the same secret.

"Hey, Glo!" called Davey's little voice through the treetops. "How you getting out to get over to the apricot boys?"

He'd been hanging around me like a mosquito buzzing in my ear, asking me this and that about how we were going to sneak out ever since he got wind of it. Every time I had to go dig, I had to shake Davey off my heels somehow. Last thing I needed was anyone from the team thinking that taking me on meant taking Davey on, too.

"So how you getting out? No one's told me nothing."

I plucked a peach. "That's top secret, kid."

"Well, if you need me, I could be a lookout! I could run reconnaissance!"

"What the heck's *reconnaissance?*"

"'S what spies do," he chirped.

The last person I wanted doing reconnaissance for me was Davey. But I did wonder if I could at least get him to fill the rest of the wheelbarrow up for me. Maybe if he finished up here I could practice at the edge of camp before the curfew.

The top of his tree rustled and trembled but all I heard was his voice coming through. "Well, ain't I got a right to see the game? I'm the one who told you how to find them boys, I wanna come, not just hear about it."

I nestled my peach in my picking bag. "Give it up, Davey, it's too risky," I said. "We gotta be careful or the whole thing'll go south."

"Well, maybe the *next* game then, maybe I could be at that one, or, you know, if you're down a guy, and you need someone to fill in—"

"Jeez, Davey, you're worse than a little brother."

As soon as I'd said it I wished I hadn't. I wished I could shove the words back into my mouth. I looked to Jess to see if she'd heard me. But she was just stacking peaches in the wheelbarrow below. I reached up and pulled a few down as Davey's silence filled the air. I reckoned some of the boys must have said something similar to him.

Still, I wasn't about to tell him anything and

have him blabbing all over camp. I already knew he couldn't keep a secret. Besides, I didn't *want* to tell him. This was the first real secret I had and I didn't want to waste it on a little kid like Davey. I'd already shared it with Jess and that could've easily gone south. Thankfully she was a smooth talker.

I glanced down at the top of her head. Jess's hair was parted straight as Sunday and it hung in long braids, tight as rope, and likely to thwack you if she whipped her head just right. She was a far cry from the girl who'd scrubbed my scalp raw back in Oklahoma.

"Boy!" called one of the clipboard men. "Once you done there, you get this tree next."

"Oh, sure, Captain!" I called. I figured if they was gonna call me something I wasn't I should at least return the favor.

I pulled the last full peach from the treetop. It was rosy and warm. Just ripe enough. Just on the other side of too soft. A perfect pie peach. Pa always said the trouble with growing things is you can forget how pretty they are. But this was the kind of peach you'd put on the top of a piano for everyone to see. The kind some lady in New York or Nashville or wherever it was going would be lucky to find tucked between the ones hard as rocks and the ones that might be too bruised up. The kind you might hold in your hand for a while before you bit into it. The kind you'd run your thumb across, soft as the back of your neck. I tucked it tenderly in my pocket. This one was just too gorgeous to risk splitting open by tossing it down or losing it among all the ordinary peaches in my sack. I'd carry her down myself.

"Coming down, Jess!" I called, and she scrambled over to steady the long thin ladder that reached up into the branches. I felt for each rung with my foot. As I climbed down, it bent and swayed against the steadiness of the trunk. With each step, the ladder buckled and groaned underneath me. Grady was right about these. They were good for firewood and that was about it.

I jumped down, holding my bag to my chest to not bruise the fruit. Before I had raised myself up, someone's fingers gripped my shoulder and shoved me back. Stinking breath was in my face and the sun was blasting white into my eyes.

"You filching product?" he said.

"What? No sir, I just—"

"What you got in your pocket?"

"Nothing!"

"No stealing product. That's the rule. Give it here, or we're taking this to the top."

I felt for the peach in my pocket.

"Now, kid."

I handed it over, wishing I had meant to steal it and hidden it better.

He chucked me once under the chin.

"Aw, don't take it hard, just doing my job, same as you."

He rubbed the fruit on his shirt and then bit into it with a slurp, scanning the trees.

"Sweet Lord, I'm sick of peaches," he sighed, and threw the rest of it sidelong. It tumbled along the ground and disappeared behind the ridge of a tire track. He walked on and my right arm pulsed.

"Don't you go throwing nothing at him," Jess whispered behind me. "It ain't worth missing your game or letting on to them you're up to no good."

"I wasn't trying to steal it," I said.

"I know," Jess said, pulling the peaches out of my bag to place them gently in the wheelbarrow.

We carried the ladder over to the tree the clipboard man had pointed to. It arched through the air as we swung its upper edge to the treetop, shaking a few leaves down as it cut through the thicket. I looked up to the white-streaked blue above, singing with birds and whistling with wind.

"Go on," Jess said, "I'll hold you steady."

I shot up the thin ladder and climbed up into the sky. If I hooked one foot around the top rung and held the thin top trunk with my hand, I could just peek my eyes out over the very top of the tree. All around me were rolling waves of green, rushing and humming in the wind.

Somewhere beyond the burning scent of the spray that coated just about everything were the soft, fragrant pine needles and the rich, deep earth. And somewhere underneath that was the scent of the mountains in the distance. Maybe there were still folks sleeping under the stars up there, far away from floodlights and fences.

Before me were rows and rows of orderly treetops, if you could even call a treetop orderly. But at the edge of the fence, you could see the wild brush trying to get in, spiraling and shooting against the chain link. Beyond that wild green was the field we'd play on, and on the other side of that was an apricot orchard, no doubt bound up in more order and more rows. No doubt brimming with souls just roiling to get out. Maybe one of them was up a tree right now, just like me. Maybe even Arlon Mackie was up there, pockets filled with little golden fruit. Maybe he was staring out at the peach orchard, thinking about how they were going to beat us and not knowing about me and my right arm. Not knowing that I was good enough and clever enough to throw Terrance Bowman off his own position. It made me smile.

That, I thought, that was worth being barked at. That was worth sweating and itching. That was worth coming home and seeing your ma with her head in her hands and your pa clutching his hat. That was worth being small, and worth being wild, and worth not knowing what would happen when the peaches were picked.

And if I could win? Strike Arlon Mackie out?

I'd never ask for anything again.

There was still plenty of light in the sky. There was still time to practice, maybe try out some different whips.

I looked down to the wheelbarrow. The sorting house gave us heck if we rolled in something half-filled.

Nuts.

And then I eyed Davey.

Jess was plucking the last few to be found on the lower branches, since the clipboard men told her she was too big to be up a ladder.

I went down the ladder slowly to give me time to think on exactly what to say. Walking up to Davey, I could see the sour look on his face that I'd put there by saying no again and again.

"Tell you what, Davey," I said.

He stuck his bottom lip out and kept moving peaches around. I wanted to tell him he'd bruise them, but I needed him on my side. Some folks don't seem to mind rubbing it in when they've got someone under their thumb. But not me.

"You not gonna answer me?" I asked. "Fine. But I'm about to cut you a deal."

His lip twitched again and his hands stopped moving.

"You fill this wheelbarrow up and bring it to the sorting house yourself, I'll tell you how to get to the game tomorrow."

His face shot up into the sun, freckles dancing across his cheeks. "You will, Glo?"

"Heck yeah, I will," I said, crossing my fingers in my pocket. I could worry about putting him off later—now all I needed was to get practicing as fast as possible.

"Honest?"

"Honest, you come knock 'shave and a haircut' on seventy-two after supper and I'll tell you."

Davey's whole body was shaking like he wanted to break out into a run. I almost felt sorry for getting him so excited.

"I got this, Gloria!" Davey half shouted as he scampered up my ladder and disappeared into the green.

I heard it before I saw it. There was a sick *snap-crack* of old weathered wood and the ladder split under Davey, teetered, and fell away from the tree. I saw his face, looking down, calm, bewildered, with his fingers spread wide like they might slow his fall.

But they didn't. Jess screamed as Davey dropped down like a last peach that somehow everyone had missed, and when he hit the earth, he didn't make a sound.

Chapter Sixteen

What happened next was fierce and frantic.

Everyone heard it and everyone ran. It was like their ears were pricked all day for something breaking. And while everyone ran towards Davey, who was looking like a rag doll, I stood and let them rush around me like a river. My neck had been sweating a moment before but the air was cold and numbing now with all those grown folk screaming and little Davey lying without moving or opening his eyes.

I heard Pa yelling in the crowd, which was getting thicker and more and more worked up. He crashed through, pulling and shoving. I just listened to the hollow space in my chest. And then Pa sprang back out of the crowd, spinning around every which way, calling "Glo!" until he saw me and grabbed me up like I wasn't just standing stuck in the earth like a hollowed-out fence post.

Pa's arms were tight around me and the beginning of his beard was rough against my face. His hands were grabbing at my hair and he kept saying, "I thought that was you, Gloria, I thought that was you!" Over his shoulder I watched them pick little Davey up and scream at one of the clipboard men to get a doctor. I knew I should feel something, knowing he was alive enough to call a doctor for. But the grown folks' noises just bounced around inside me until they ran out of steam.

And then Ma was up behind me, wrapping her arms around me and Pa at the same time, saying, "She's all right, Silas, she's here, we're all right." But Pa was shaking as much as I was still and it was Ma's arms that were holding strong and holding us up. We stood for a while, and I saw Jess standing a ways off just looking like she wasn't sure whether to hold on to Ma or whether she ought to just keep her distance and let Pa's shaking and muttering pass.

When Pa finally set me down it was like when you fall out of a dream and jerk yourself awake. Sounds got clearer in my brain and the hollow space started filling back up again. I could see Davey's ladder, with the top two rungs split and a toppled wheelbarrow of fruit I'd asked him to fill for me. I looked at where Davey had been as Ma and Pa started talking angry. At the orchard, at the clipboard men, at California, at everything, didn't even seem like they cared if someone heard them. Pa kept his hand gripping my shoulder tight while he talked.

"Hey, Gloria," Jess said. Her voice was soft and sad, the way it had been the morning Yvette and Rosalita had to go.

"He all right?" I said. My voice was like molasses, pouring out slow.

"I saw him breathing," Jess said.

"Aw, well, that's good."

I said it like Jess had found a lost button, or gotten the top off a jar.

She shrugged a little too quickly and we started walking back towards number 72 with Davey's fall hanging over us like a bad secret. I wondered if anyone had heard me tell him to go up that ladder. I wondered if Davey's ma would find out I'd egged him on. I wondered if she'd come hollering at our door.

It was a like a sea of bad churning up my insides.

But the worst part of it was this wormy little feeling that I was glad it had been Davey to fall, and not me.

• • •

We ate quietly. A couple times Pa asked us to repeat exactly what the clipboard men had said about the treetops being for littler ones. Mostly Jess talked. And Pa sat there listening like a wire was pulling tighter and tighter across his ribs. And Ma sat there still as a cat watching at the window. She was holding herself together but I could tell a wound had broken open inside her, maybe from Davey falling. Or maybe from realizing it might have been me. I just sat there trying not to see Davey falling again and again. Kicking myself for telling him to go up that ladder in the first place.

Downright dumb. Downright selfish.

When a knock came at the door, Pa just stood quietly and opened it up like we'd been expecting someone all along. In stepped a fellow looking a little younger than Pa, no hat on his head, smelling of spray and sweat. As he came into the light, I saw he was the man that was always next to the girl in the faded pink dress with the baby.

"Did anyone see you?" Pa asked.

"No, sir," said the man. He turned to Ma. "Name's Blight, Sam Blight."

"Quite a name for a farmer," Ma said, folding a dish towel in her lap.

"Not a farmer anymore," he said. "Your kids okay?"

Ma nodded. "My girl was up the same tree not a minute before. You got kids here?"

Sam raked his fingers across his cheek. "A little one. Just a baby. Too small to be climbing. But the spray on the peaches ain't good for him, or his ma. Can't barely breathe."

The corner of Ma's lip twitched like that wound in her scratched open a little more.

"Anyway, that's why I'm here," Sam said. "I swear to God, if that had been my kid—"

Ma dropped the folded dish towel on the table. "My girls have heard enough swearing today, Mr. Blight."

He nodded and said, "Ma'am," dipping his head with his word.

"You talk to the others?" Pa said, stepping in close.

Sam Blight looked to me and Jess and then back to Pa. He nodded once.

"All right then," said Pa as Ma handed him his coat. "Jess, Glo, mind your ma and go to bed."

He didn't wait for a reply. He and Sam Blight stepped out into the dark, past curfew and everything.

"Silas?" Ma called, calm and cool.

Pa ducked his head back in.

"Don't you get caught," she said.

He smiled. "On my honor, Evelyne."

I wasn't sure how you could promise to not get caught. If it was that easy, I'd have been making promises like that every day of my life. But when Pa stepped back out, I felt at least a little sure that he'd come back. It was the way he said it that made me believe it.

Jess was already settling down in bed. When Ma shut the light off, Jess's hand squeezed mine. The world went quiet and soon I could hear Ma's sleep breathing. But I was stuck on the surprised look on Davey's face when he fell. Like he was dreaming and had forgotten he was up a tree. I said a prayer to make me fall asleep quick.

Either I was dead tired or God was listening.

I opened up my eyes to the strange sight of mid-morning light beaming through the window. Jess was standing, looking out, the light making a halo of her hair. I rolled onto my side and pressed myself up, groaning like an old gate. When I pressed my eyes together I saw Davey flying down to earth, and even when I opened them I could still hear the thud. It made me want to press myself into a tiny ball and pull the covers over my head.

"Morning," I croaked.

Jess spun around and a thousand words tumbled out of her mouth.

"You up, Glo? Ma said to let you sleep. Said you and me weren't picking today. Just resting. Folks are saying that ladder never should've been out. Saying they knew the ladders were no good, that's why they were telling the kids to use 'em. They're saying Davey's got no broken bones, but they'll be good and bruised. Says if he wakes up he's in the clear, but he ain't yet—"

"Pa come back?"

"He was here this morning. Dunno when he came in."

As I stood, the blood rushed to my head and I saw stars for a moment. Must've slept like the dead.

"Everyone's talking about it," Jess whispered. "Everyone's talking about how they put a kid on a bad piece of equipment. Everybody's real mad. Everybody's saying they gotta do something, but I don't know what they're gonna do."

I went to the window. The sun was high in the sky, warmth baking off the sill. As I stared at the shadowless ground, a rope wrapped around my ribs and pulled tight. I knew I had to get to the game, but I felt rotten. The last thing I wanted was to have folks staring at me.

"Glo . . . ?"

"Yeah, Jess?"

"Don't we—I mean, don't you gotta get to the game?"

I hoisted one of my overall straps up. "Sure, yeah," I said.

Something hopeful stirred in Jess's face as she said, "Oh, good! I was worried that you—Well, I thought maybe you might not . . . you know . . . after yesterday."

"What about yesterday?" I snapped.

"Nothing . . . I just . . . well, I guess we gotta *go*."

I felt like I was looking at Jess through muddy water. I could see her jitters, and the way she kept looking from me to the door and back again. She didn't want to get to the game. She wanted to get to Joe Franklin's sweet son. Finally she grabbed my hand and yanked me towards the door.

"Gloria, we gotta go, we gotta go *right now*!"

"All right!" I barked back, and we were off, slinking through camp like alley cats. This was all wrong. My head felt full of cotton and my ribs hurt from holding my breath. I wasn't sure what I hated more: the fact that it was my fault Davey had fallen, or the fact that I might be late to my own game.

We darted through the trees, ran deep into the center of the Santa Ana Holdsten Peach Orchard so we could come out the other side to where the fence met the wild. When we got to the bend in the fence, we cleared away the brush that one of the boys had left to keep it secret. I could see that they all had been through here. The fence was bent up even more. Probably for Clyde. They had all come through here.

I was last.

Jess and I shimmied under the fence like snakes and popped out the other side, dusty.

"Quentin said to follow the creek," Jess said. "We just got to follow the creek to get there—"

"I know, Jess!" I hollered. It came out angry and broken and a little mean. But my head was swimming, asking Davey to go up that ladder and watching him fall.

And then, through the grasses, I could hear them. Oh Lord, I could hear them! They were either done or hadn't started yet.

I started running.

"Glo, *wait!*" Jess called.

But I was hurtling towards the opening in the tall grasses, smacking the long leaves out of my face like I was clearing brush. I burst out, stopping to catch my breath and holding on as a wave of dizziness that I'd outrun caught up with me and filled my head with sloshing water and my ears with cotton. For a moment I couldn't hear or see, but then it was like mud settling in a pond, and a chorus of whoops and hollers came up as the boys—as *my team*—ran up around me. Behind them, the apricot boys stood watching and trying to figure me out. And standing on the pitcher's mound, looking like I'd pulled the rug out from under him, was Terrance.

"Glo, where you been? You get caught or something? We thought you were gonna be a no-show!" said Clyde.

"Nah," I said, "not me!"

Quentin rushed up. "How's Davey? How's he doing?"

Fast falling. Quiet as a shooting star. Sound like a sack of grain hitting the earth.

"Hasn't woken up yet, but no broken bones," I said, turning to Jess. But she was nowhere in sight. Probably making her way through the smattering of kid spectators looking for a boy who smiled too much.

"I ain't playing with no girl!" I heard someone call.

"She don't even *look* like a girl!" someone else called.

"Peaches playing with *girls* now!" someone laughed. A chorus of whistles and kissy noises followed and I felt small. I had heard this a million times. And it usually bounced right off me. But now, each word was a stone socked right into my gut. I shot my eyes over to Terrance. He was just standing there, nose wrinkled up to the sky, like he'd seen this all coming a million miles away.

"Hey now," came a voice long and cool like a tall glass of water. The noises stopped on a dime.

A lanky boy, freckled and golden and swimming in clothes too wide for him, stepped towards me. Apricot boy. His thumbs hooked into his pockets, and he stood wide like a cowboy. Whatever commotion I'd drummed up, he'd stopped with a word and a stance. Behind him I could see the other apricot boys leaning in and listening.

"So it's true some kid's knocked out from some bum ladder?"

I nodded because my words went with the wind and were probably caught in some tree somewhere.

"'S true," I muttered.

The lanky boy's face twisted up like he was counting steps between him and the clouds.

"It's like they *want* all hell to break loose," he said. "Orchard might as well be made of dynamite. All she needs is someone with a matchbook."

I heard the breeze whistling above.

The boy traced the tip of one long foot in the dirt and winked back up at me. "So you're the one who kicked Terrance Bowman off his pitcher's mound?"

A rustle of snickers sounded behind him.

"Sure am," I said.

Normally I would've gone on about my arm this and my arm that, but words that had come easy with the peach orchard boys were too much for me to chew on here and now.

"Well, I didn't come here to chitchat," said the golden boy. "I came here to play ball. What's your name, kid?"

This was the time to swagger. This was the time to boast. This was the time to wink. But all that came out of me was a tiny "Gloria Mae Willard."

The boy held out a hand with fingers long and knobby.

"Name's Mackie. Arlon Mackie. Let's get to it."

Chapter Seventeen

"Come on, Gloria!" shouted Jess, even though she was barely looking at me. She was sitting alone on the grass, looking every which way for Joe Franklin's sweet son. I was surprised she even noticed I was batting.

I was on my second strike and we were two outs. I wasn't a great hitter, but I wasn't usually this bad.

"Come on, Glo!" shouted Clyde from third base. All I had to do was hit halfway decent and we'd get a run. But if I was out, no more chance of scoring.

I could tell by the look on Terrance's face he was enjoying watching me sweat just a little. He wanted to see me get a taste of losing after Arlon said I was the girl who knocked him off his high horse. As the apricot boys whistled around me, clapping and hollering for their side to get me out and get me out good, it struck me that Terrance was wanting to see me knocked down a notch myself, even if it meant he went down with me.

I held the bat tighter like that might make the difference. I couldn't be soft. I couldn't be weak. "Come on, Glo," I whispered to myself. I was staring hard at their pitcher, who had a pleased look on his face, like it was some kind of novelty to be pitching to a girl. I wanted to tell him to just hurry up and throw already. He grinned at me and I heard the catcher behind him snicker and—

Thunk!

"Strike three!"

My skin felt prickly and breath was catching at my throat.

"Hold your head up, Glo," I whispered as we moved to the outfield.

Quentin ran past me on his way out, calling, "Knock 'em dead, Gloria!" like he actually believed it would happen.

I wasn't so sure. The apricot boys were all taller, surer, prouder, and faster. I'd been watching them in the outfield. They moved together like they were part of the same creature. They were fast and focused and laughed easy and clapped each other on the back every chance they got. And all Arlon had to do was chuckle and the rest of them started laughing like they all knew something we didn't.

We, on the other hand, were keeping our distance from each other, like nervous cats. Or at least, me and Terrance were.

This wasn't exactly how I'd imagined my first game. I'd imagined Pa and Ma there. I certainly never thought *Jess* would be my only fan. But she wasn't much interested in the game anyway. Even she didn't really want to be here.

If Davey were here, he'd be cheering me louder than anyone. He'd have brought his bottle caps to show me, followed me to the game, followed me home.

An apricot boy whistled and I turned to see a ball shooting through the air at me like they wanted to knock the wind out of me.

Slap!

The feel of the ball in my hand kicked me out of my mind and onto the field. I caught it easy in my right hand and gave the thrower a look that could have singed the tips off the grass. He put his arms up and stepped back.

My turn.

There was a sprinkling of clapping from the other apricot kids who were looking on. Terrance was over on the left side of the field just a stone's throw away. He laughed at something they said and one of the kids pointed my way.

Doggone stupid laughing boys.

I planted my feet down into the ground to steady myself on the pulse of the earth. This was *my* game. Sure, it wasn't what I thought it'd be. But I'd fought to get here and I'd earned my place. I belonged here. Still, I couldn't help looking around me at the sea of boys. And I didn't know which ones really wanted me there. Quentin did, that was clear. Clyde seemed like he did. They all had the day before when I'd been helping them dig. Maybe it was harder to want me here now that the apricot boys could see they had a girl on their team. Maybe I didn't want to be here myself with all those eyes looking at me.

Somewhere behind me I could swear I heard someone say "skirt" and "girlie."

"Shut up!" I yelled.

It made it worse. They all went, *"Ooooooooh!"*

If Davey were here he would've stood and tried to blow one of those ear-piercing whistles to drown them out. Lord, I was rotten. Lord, I'd been selfish. It was what Pa had been trying to say all along.

You just can't—you can't be this way, Gloria. Maybe if I'd listened to him there wouldn't be a busted-up kid lying back at camp with his ma whispering prayers over him.

An apricot kid was coming up to home plate, marked by a beat-up old washboard. He was smiling at me, grinning like he had a ten-dollar bill in his pocket. I wondered if they'd lined up their easiest guys, or their toughest, or if they hadn't thought about it at all, which somehow made it worse. I gripped the ball, the pads of my fingers pressing into the ridges of the stitching, wound it back, and launched it forwards.

The air hissed as the apricot boy swung a second too late for my fastball. The ten-dollar bill in his pocket had turned into a fiver.

Casey tossed the ball back to me, and even though there was still snickering behind me coming from those darn apricot spectators, it was piercing through my skin just a little bit less.

You're worse than a little brother.

Thud.

Focus.

The boy with the bat hiked it up over his shoulders and nodded at me. He'd be expecting something fast this time. He'd be thinking I was too dumb to know that. But I wasn't. I wound it back same as I had before but sent it long and easy, like I was helping Clyde practice his swing.

This time the boy swung a second too soon. He was down to one lousy buck, and the apricot boys were paying attention now like a cat that sees its mouse still has some spunk.

One more.

Casey tossed me the ball. The chittering behind me had thankfully stopped. Not that I was gonna let that bother me. I stood tall with the ball behind my back, fixing my grip to throw it curved. No one was gonna laugh at me after this. I wound it up fast so he couldn't see where my fingers were at and launched it forwards, snapping the end of my wrist so the ball curved in a delicious arc that he missed by a foot.

I heard the scattered cheering from my team in the outfield, and I could see Casey bouncing in his seat. Arlon had leaned forward from his perch like things had gotten real interesting.

"Just you wait, Arlon," I said to myself.

I watched as Arlon stepped easily forward and took the bat off his teammate.

Well then.

He was taller even than Clyde and as he walked up to the plate, the whole field tensed and rippled. I heard the word "skirt" again behind me, but I figured those apricot boys were saying it now because they were scared of me. Meanness is funny like that. The bigger you get the smaller they have to make you feel.

Arlon stretched his arms up, the bat making him even taller, and then he swung them down, sending the bat around in a graceful arc before he swung it back up over his shoulder like a knapsack he'd been carrying his whole life.

I'd be lying if I said my heart hadn't gone just a little haywire, even with the boost of the last out making it beat strong and steady.

I could do this. I just had to strike one player out. Just one. Just Arlon Mackie. If I struck him out, I knew I could pitch a perfect game from here on in. And if I didn't . . . I couldn't think about that.

"Get her, Arlon!" someone called.

"Get him, Glo!" Rudy called from behind me. "Show him what you got!"

I took a breath, breathed in the air, hot and gritty but free and wide.

And then behind me I heard someone making kissy noises. I knew what Ma would say, *Leave them be. Show them you're bigger by not playing their game*—but that was just it. This was *my* game and they were mucking it up. Time to put those apricot pits in their place. Mid–kissy noise I swung around so they'd know I knew and there—

There was Terrance. Leaning into their laughter. Terrance had been making fun of me. Terrance had been, as Quentin might say, *consorting with the enemy*. He blinked up at me and shrugged.

The scheming, two-faced son of a gun. The earth pulse got louder and more angry. I wanted to throw the baseball square at his head.

"Don't you muck this up, Gloria," I hissed under my breath, turning back to Arlon.

He was smiling like a jack-o'-lantern.

I could do this. Wipe that smile off Arlon's face and steal Terrance's laughter right outta his lungs. The anger was making me quake.

I hitched my left leg up and cranked my arm back. I wound it up and shot everything I had into my right arm. And maybe it was the anger and maybe it was that sound Davey made when he landed or maybe I just wasn't as good as I thought, because I saw that ball sail through the air and could even hear Arlon laugh right before he smacked it all the way into the sun.

Chapter Eighteen

"It doesn't matter."

That was what Quentin said to me after the game. And on the way back to camp, he was the only one to walk near me. The rest of the boys huddled around Terrance. Probably talking about what a bad idea it was to let me play. Probably talking about taking a vote to kick me out. Soon as we were through the hole in the fence, I ducked between the trees. Didn't want to see a soul.

"It don't matter," said Jess that evening, still rosy from the sun. "And if it makes you feel any better, I didn't find who I was looking for."

It didn't make me feel any better.

And it did matter.

It did and she knew it.

I felt sore about it. All of it. And when I walked back into camp I started praying Davey'd come running up to me, grinning through a nasty bruise or two. That was about the only thing I could think of that might pluck the sting out of the day. And if he *did* come running, I'd tell him everything. Sit him down, let him show me his bottle caps, tell him he could come next Sunday, tell him I'd teach him to throw better.

But he didn't.

I wasn't even interested in what was happening when Sam Blight showed up to meet with Pa after dark. I just crawled into bed and shut my eyes tight until I disappeared into sleep. Now the early-morning sun was white and the air crisp. My brain was full of falling and losing and for once I was glad to be small.

Easier to miss in the crowd.

I did my best to disappear as we all walked towards the orchard after the morning alarm sounded. People were tired, people were restless, and I was aching.

But even with all the stinging in my brain, I could tell something was different today.

Since we'd come to the Santa Ana Holdsten

Peach Orchard, all of the pickers had been walking around like they were ashamed. But now they were straight and tall as fence posts. And that wasn't all. The men with the clipboards were all jumpy as cats in a room full of rocking chairs as they watched us head towards the orchard. I heard Sam Blight whisper to Pa that even the man who ran the company store had taken to nervously cleaning his pistol on the counter when anyone walked in.

We came to a restless stop in front of the orchard, and it was clear we were going to hear from the California Growers Association man again. I could see him standing off to the side, eyes darting about and hand fishing around in the pocket of his waistcoat.

As we waited to hear what he had to say, Ma put her hand on my shoulder.

"Listen up," she said. "I know I'm always telling you to mind grown folk. But if one of those men tells you to get up on one of those ladders, you come straight to me. I'll deal with him myself."

A ripple of grumbles and almost-growls went through the standing crowd as the man with the plum-colored silk on his hat stepped up. He had a megaphone this time, like he knew he was gonna have to fight to be heard. As he took a crisp handkerchief to dab his brow, I felt Pa's anger coming off him like heat off pavement. Ma's hands had gone to her hips and she began slowly shaking her head from side to side, watching him like a cat. Everyone shifted back and forth a bit until the man's voice called out—

"Now, now, I can see you're upset about what happened yesterday. Heck, I'm upset. But this is farmwork, accidents happen—"

A groan went up from the crowd like steam.

"*Accidents happen.* And by God, this valley is crawling with no-good scum looking to take advantage of what happened here yesterday to get good, honest Americans talking Red—"

The groan was becoming a snarl and the crowd was pulsing together.

"We've had troublemakers here before and we are not afraid to *deal with them*—"

The crowd was rumbling as a group, one single thronging buzz, and the man with the plum-colored silk sent his voice booming.

"But I don't think we'll have a problem here, oh no. I've seen riffraff looking for handouts, I've seen bindle stiffs who don't know a hard day's work, and I've seen lowlifes who didn't seem to know you've got to put in a little sweat to make a dime here in the great state of California. But I don't see that here. I see folks who want honest work. You aren't riffraff, you aren't bindle stiffs, you aren't lowlifes. You're decent Americans."

A memory flashed through my mind of the bank man back in Oklahoma. Calm and still and offering Pa one of the long white cigarettes he held in a silver case while pulling the land out from underneath us. He might've even shaken Pa's hand if I hadn't gone and busted up his car. Just like the bank man, the white-suit man was buttering us up while holding us down. And just like back in Balko, there wasn't a grown folk in the place about to stand up to it.

And then a voice cut through the air, clear and high as a church bell.

"If we so decent, why we making sixteen cents an hour? If we so decent, how come my wife's paying three times what food's worth in the company store? If we so decent, how come we got kids who been climbing trees their whole life falling fifteen feet 'cause of a bum ladder? What's so decent about that?"

The crowd's roar had turned to a holy sort of humming, and it was like the wind was at our back, like someone had just pointed to a way forwards, like someone had just said what was on everyone's mind, like someone was finally standing up and—

And it was Pa. It was my pa. Pa, who'd signed over everything we owned. Pa, who'd told me to keep in line. Pa, who'd always said we had to keep on keeping on. Pa, who always kept out of trouble. Pa, who'd told me all we had to do was put in our time, give a little sweat, and we'd get ahead. Here he was standing up, just one lone soul in a crowd of others who were itching to do what he did but couldn't.

And behind him was Sam Blight, nodding and standing next to his wife and little baby. He was watching the folks around him react. Maybe they'd planned this. Maybe not.

But almost everyone in the crowd was looking at my pa. Nodding at him. And a near-dead ember flickered on inside, me growing brighter with each breath I took. But as the crowd began to flicker on, too, the clipboard men started looking more angry than nervous. And this time the man from the California Growers Association was barking like a dog.

"Now listen, you all been told there's no organizing here, or anywhere for that matter. And believe me, whoever it is that has been spreading Red materials will be prosecuted to the fullest extent of the law. You wanna go stand in the heat asking for wages you're never gonna get? Well, that's just fine. But the next man, woman, or child that starts talking Red to me can go see if they got any room at the government camp with the other lowlifes, 'cause you will not be welcome here anymore. Now get in, start picking, or get out. Choice is yours."

The crowd bent but didn't break. We started shuffling in, but something was beating and pulsing just below the soil, drumming us up. Drumming us up, because Pa had taken a stand. I'd told too many secrets not to recognize the looks that were passing between all the grown folks. Looks that said *This isn't over yet.*

Pa walked tall and proud into the orchard with Sam darting in and out and whispering things into his ear. Ma had her hand on Pa's shoulder, and me and Jess strung along behind them like kites. She shot me a look that was caught somewhere between worried and excited and I did my best to grin.

But the thought of losing the day before was like a stone in my shoe that just wouldn't shake loose. Every time I blinked, Arlon's home-run ball shooting up high in the sky was right behind my eyelids. Every time I thought of all the boasting I had done to get on the team, it made my insides ache with shame. I wanted to disappear, melt down to the ground, and sink into the dirt.

"Hey, you," said a familiar voice between the trees.

I stopped and turned, waving Jess on ahead of me.

There, standing tall like the day I met him, was Terrence Bowman, arms crossed and eyes set and staring.

I stood there, looking at him, no words at the ready. Nothing to do but tense up for whatever he was gonna throw my way. And whatever he threw was gonna hurt.

"So is it just you and your pa, or do big mouths run in your family?"

"Dunno what you mean," I said, keeping my head down.

"You know darn well what I mean. You come in here, talking a mile a minute, kicking me out, saying you can do this and you can do that. All you got is a good story, there's nothing to it."

I looked up. "I struck out some of their guys, didn't I?"

"You got lucky."

The earth was pulsing hot underneath me again.

"I didn't get lucky," I said, "I practiced. I practiced all my life and every day from Oklahoma to here."

"Oh yeah? You practiced? Well, I did, too. You know what else I did? I got the team together, I got us organized, I got us playing, and I'm the one who snuck out and got the apricot boys playing, too—"

"You were standing there snickering at me!

You're supposed to watch my back, you're supposed to be on my team!"

"Sure, yeah, I was snickering at you, the whole field was snickering at you—"

"Well, you shouldn't've!"

"Well, I did, stop being so sore about it! If I had a nickel for every name I been called, I sure wouldn't be picking peaches right now! Or ain't you used to folks being tough on you?"

I started walking and Terrence fell in right beside me.

"I got us everything we got. And you come in thinking you can just claim what you want by talking foolish."

The heat was coming up from the ground and burning the bottoms of my feet.

"I ain't foolish."

"You bad luck, Gloria, and whatever your pa and that Blight man are cooking up has bad luck written all over it."

Our voices jostled with each step, and we were trying not to be too loud, but anger was pressing against my throat like a horse in a burning stable.

"My pa stood up for everyone."

"Your pa is gonna get everyone's head split open."

"Don't you say that!"

"It's true, I seen this all before. This is just the way it was with Jimmy's pa. And Grady, too."

I whipped my head around. "You just saying that 'cause you ashamed you didn't do nothing for Jimmy's pa! Y'all just let him get beat. Your friend's pa! 'Cause you didn't have the guts to—"

"You're too dumb to see that one minute your pa'll be talking high and mighty, next minute he'll be picking his own teeth up off the floor of a jail cell. Ain't nothing any of us can do about it."

Something reared up inside me. "Don't you say something like that *about my pa*."

"Or maybe it don't matter 'cause he don't have what it takes just like you don't have what it takes and this whole thing is gonna fizzle out."

"I got what it takes. He got what it takes!"

"You just watch, this will fall apart just like you on that pitching mound! I hope they throw you outta this place!"

"You a bully!"

"You a liar and loser!"

"Yeah well, at least my ma thinks I'm worth sticking around for!"

He stopped. We were both breathing hard and staring the other one down. I watched as the muscles around his eyes twitched and tightened.

He hurled himself at me and slammed me into

the back of a tree. My arms flew out, grabbing for air, and for a moment I wasn't sure where my elbows and knees ended and his started. The side of my face hit dirt and the thrumming in the earth surged up into my right arm as my fist met Terrance's jaw. He jerked back, stunned as me, and then he knocked me good in the same spot, sending white flashes spiraling up through my vision.

And then there were strong arms wrenching us apart and an ice-cold shock of water drenching me. I stood up and back, shaking the water out of my eyes as a clamor of grown men yelled at us to *Get! Get on back!*

So I did. Holding the side of my face, I backed away from my tussling spot as Terrance backed away from his until the trees closed up around me like a net.

Chapter Nineteen

Ma pressed the cool rag to my cheek. I wasn't
sure what she'd heard about what happened, but she
just tended to me like I'd scraped my knee, not like
I'd gotten socked in the face, after doing some sock-
ing myself. Picking was done for the day after hours
looking and whispering and nodding, and the word
"strike" was getting tossed around from ear to ear.
Something was about to happen. But just like every
time, no one was about to tell me anything.

"Hold that there," Ma said gently, and I took
the rag and pressed it.

I'd been looking at the floor. Waiting for her to
say something like *Wait for your father to get home*

or *Gloria. Mae. Willard.* But she just sat down and crossed her legs on me and Jess's thin little mattress and put her chin in her hands, looking at me, calm as the sky after a storm. I couldn't remember the last time we'd been alone like this. Part of me wanted Jess or Pa to burst through the door. Part of me hoped they wouldn't.

We sat there in the puzzling quiet until I asked, "What are you thinking, Ma?"

She took a deep breath.

"I'm thinking . . . that I hope you never know what it's like to see your child get hurt. I don't wish that on anyone."

"Not even that man from the California Growers Association?"

"Not even him."

I could tell she meant it. And I felt bad for hurting her by getting myself hurt. I'd always wondered how Ma kept on keeping on. With every storm back in Oklahoma, tying damp rags around our faces, with the first bad crop, and the second, and the third, with listening to Little Si struggle to breathe and then watching him die. And having to be strong all the same. I always thought it meant she didn't feel things as hard. And I was thinking now I was wrong about that.

I looked out the little window of our shanty. Out

there was electricity, humming, pulsing, and whis-pering. In here it was soft and gentle and still, like when you let yourself sink to the bottom of a pond.

"So," Ma said, reading my thoughts, "you want to tell me what started all this?"

I wanted to talk about something else, just in case I broke. But as Ma looked at me, I felt the truth start to fill up my belly and then my lungs. It was clear and cold, like a hidden spring, coming up and up.

And then, out the truth came, spilling over everything.

Ma sat, hands folded together, composed and quiet as a preacher's wife. She let the quiet fill up the room, swirling around us. I told her about meeting Terrance and the team and how he told me I couldn't play. I told her about how I would've struck Clyde out if Terrance had given me the chance. I told her about how Terrance was mean on account of his ma having left. I told her about our secret meeting and the plan to loosen the dirt under the fence so we could slide under. I told her about losing to Arlon Mackie after I said I'd help us win. I told her what Terrance had said about Pa and how I boiled over. I told her he might've pushed me first, but it was me who threw the first punch.

When I was done I was soggy and spent. But

there was part of the story I hadn't said out loud. The part I was ashamed of. The part I couldn't bear to say. Ma leaned in and touched my knee with the tips of her fingers.

"What'd you say? Right before you threw punches?"

The words formed a knot in my throat and part of me wanted to keep them there forever, tied up and hidden. But Ma's gaze was pulling the horrible thing up and out.

"I said . . . I said at least my ma thinks I'm worth sticking around for."

It hurt to say out loud, but once the words left my lips it was like stones lifted off my shoulders.

Ma breathed in and out slowly. "Aw, Gloria . . . ," she sighed.

I looked at my hands, grubby and lined with dark dirt.

"Where'd that come from?" Ma asked, tucking a piece of hair behind my ear.

"He put me down," I said. "I'm tired of people putting me down. I'm tired of people thinking they don't want me around—I'm tired of—"

"Who doesn't want you around?"

"No one. Everyone's always telling me to shove off, and stay out of it—"

"I want you around."

"Yeah, but—"

"Pa wants you around."

"Well, then he should—"

"Jess wants you around."

I swallowed. "Well then—I dunno, I just—"

"Sounds like a lot of those boys wanted you around."

"Well, I don't wanna take things lying down. I ain't like you and Pa and Jess, who can just keep going when someone's robbing you blind, and laughing in your face—"

"That how you see it?"

"Well, *yeah*. And maybe you can let it all roll off you, but I got pride. And—and—he was hurting my pride so I . . ."

I trailed off.

"Pride's a funny thing," Ma said. "It makes people do funny things. Like what you did today. I'd rather my daughter had some honor than have her pride."

"Ain't that the same thing?"

Ma shook her head. "Pride makes you do foolish things you regret later. Like hurting someone when you could talk it out. Honor . . . well, it's got more to do with doing the right thing, even when it's hard."

"You mean like striking?"

Ma looked up, surprised. "A little bit like that, yes."

She let that one sit, simmering in the warm air.

"So . . . are we striking?" I asked.

Ma stared back at me. "What do you think?"

I pulled my knees up to my chest. "I think Pa and that Blight man are planning something."

The look on Ma's face told me everything I needed to know.

"It's only gonna work if everyone feels the same way as your pa and Mr. Blight," she said.

"But don't they?"

Ma sighed. "Sure, folks are mad and folks want better. But they're also scared. And being scared makes it hard to do the right thing."

"So then you gotta make folks *not* scared."

"You gotta give them a reason to believe that things will be better if they drum up some courage, but . . . sometimes folks are happy to stay where they are as long as someone's underneath them. Makes them feel like things aren't as bad as they are when there's folks to look down on."

I thought of Davey and keeping him at arm's length. I thought of the way the man from the California Growers Association talked about folks at government camps, about Michelson's.

"And," Ma added, "that makes folks think they're

just a step away from being a boss themselves. Or they think the boss is just doing what is natural for a boss to do. Shoot, that's what Pa was saying when we got here."

"But he's not saying that now."

Ma's mouth twitched up and she looked back at me with a ghost of a smile on her face. "No, Gloria, I knocked some sense into him."

"You did?"

She nodded.

"Ma, *you* talked him into this? You a radical now?"

Ma's head jerked back.

"No one in this family is a radical, Gloria, least of all me."

I nodded, even though I was pretty sure we all were at that point.

"I tell you one thing, Gloria, if we do strike, it's gonna happen soon. Mr. Blight says you gotta strike while the iron is hot. I don't disagree."

Ma looked off behind me. She stared into space like she was looking for something.

"Sometimes I don't know where Mr. Blight gets it from," she said. "You'd think a man with a tiny baby and wife wouldn't be so ready to put it all on the line."

"And you ready to put it all on the line?"

Ma traced the tip of her finger along a line of faded daisies on the sheet.

"I don't know. But you're right about something, Gloria. When you don't fight for what you deserve, the world just digs its heel into you a little bit more. If you don't speak up for yourself, probably no one else will. But," she said, taking my chin in her hand, "speaking up is different than tearing down."

The peace in the room was as fine and delicate as a spider's web. I'd made it this far without breaking. I'd felt rotten, I'd felt ashamed, but I hadn't broken. I was tired, though. And I wanted to be able to be alone with my ma again, anytime I wanted. I didn't want to worry about what was behind her eyes, or think about what was on her mind. I didn't want her to keep things from me, and I didn't want to keep things from her. I'd spent so much time wanting to show I didn't need help, that I was fine on my own. Maybe she'd been doing the same thing.

"Ma . . . ," I said slowly.

Her eyes drifted up to mine, deep pools of calm.

"How come you didn't fight for us to stay in Oklahoma? How come you didn't speak up for us when the bank man came?"

Ma's eyes got deeper and her shoulders melted down. "Aw, Gloria," she said. "You couldn't have paid me a million dollars to keep on living in a house that my baby died in."

My chest collapsed and a sob came rattling out of my lungs, wet and raw. It was loud. Surprising. And then uncontrollable, raking across my ribs, skipping and halting on its way out. But Ma looked like she'd been expecting it. And she took me in her arms, a summer warmth all around me, pressing me into stillness. All I could smell was her sun-baked skin. All I could hear was the soft pound of her heartbeat. And there were her hands lacing through my hair. There was her voice softly saying *"Shh . . . ,"* which was the sweetest thing I'd ever heard.

When I finally pulled back there was a gentle smile on Ma's lips. She held my face in her two hands and tucked my hair behind my ears.

"You've got a good heart, Gloria. You're just figuring out how to use it. It's something most folks never learn to do. If they did, none of us would be in the spot we're in now."

I reached down and tugged at the laces on my boot. I was sore all over. My jaw from Terrance's fist and my fist from Terrance's jaw. But most of all it was my heart that was sore. It ached with each beat, but it was alive and strong and thumping up ideas into my brain.

"I think I gotta go, Ma. I won't be long."

She nodded and watched me as I pulled my cap back on my head and stumbled up to stand.

"Gloria . . ."

"Yeah, Ma?"

"You know I'm still gonna have to talk to Pa about this. About you ducking work and sneaking around. 'Bout you keeping secrets."

Part of me got ready to fight back. Say that Pa didn't trust me with his business so why should I trust him with mine? But Ma's words about honor were still whispering about in the air.

"All right," I said. And with that, Ma stood and started mixing up supper.

Walking across camp, I could hear all the mas whispering behind the lines of hanging laundry, all the pas counting the coins in the tiny cans they were storing under the floorboards, all the kids that were whispering about how little Davey was doing and who'd seen the fistfight between me and Terrance. I wondered just who was in each shanty, who was too scared to strike, who still thought sixteen cents an hour was a sure path to their own piece of land.

I walked and walked, my heart thumping louder and louder the closer I got to Terrance Bowman's cabin. The world around me was busying and moving fast, but I must have stared at his door forever before I reached out and knocked "shave and a haircut."

"Here goes nothing," I said.

Chapter Twenty

The inside of Terrance's shanty was a mess of hanging socks and the smell of laundry far gone. Old empty cans of beans were stacked in the corner and when Terrance threw an old dish towel over them so I wouldn't see, the air came alive with flies. There were clothes, like a sort of nest in the corner, and a thin, dirty little mattress in the middle of the room. The place stank like old whiskey and heartache.

"Where's your pa?" I asked, real quiet.

"Out," Terrance replied with a bark.

"Oh," I said. "Right."

The air was sour and not just from the smell. The

weight of it was filling my lungs up with awful.

"I shouldn't've said that," I blurted, "about your ma. It was wrongheaded and mean and I shouldn't've done it."

"Yeah, well," he said.

I'd come in meaning to apologize, but also expecting an apology in return. He'd started it, hadn't he? But standing in the middle of Terrance's cabin made me wonder if I didn't already have enough of everything else, and if needing an apology was asking for just a little too much. Our place wasn't much to look at but it wasn't . . . this. And Terrance was being tight-lipped, for sure, but I wondered if maybe he was just a little embarrassed, too, with me seeing how he and his pa lived. His breath started going all funny like he was trying to find the right words to sweeten the air or at least stop it from feeling like it was bearing down on us.

"You shouldn't—" he started, "you shouldn't— you just—you shouldn't kick a guy when he's down."

I could see his own truth bubbling up, just like mine had done with Ma. And just like Ma had done, I figured I should just be quiet and let it come.

"You don't know," he said, "you don't know anything about me. Or what I been through. You got everything. And all I got was my team, that I made, and then you just—you just come in—and all right, you're good, but why you gotta take the only thing I got?"

I blinked.

"You think you got it so tough, but you don't," he said. "You don't know nothing about tough."

I did know something about tough. I carried tough in my pockets like stones. But I also knew that Terrance had something he needed to get off his chest. And right now, I just needed to listen.

"And you're a girl. And no one is expecting you to—to—to just—look, things are just *different* for you."

I wanted to tell him I was about as good at doing girl things as Quentin was at playing baseball. But that seemed beside the point.

"And my ma *didn't* run off 'cause of me or my pa, she run off 'cause things got bad and she didn't want to see 'em get worse. And *that's* why he—that's why, so— Well, that's just the truth."

His words made his face and everything he'd ever done or said to me burn in bright, clear focus. I'd spent so much time wanting to prove myself, I didn't realize Terrance was doing the same thing. Trying to make it seem like there was nothing raw and half-ruined underneath. We'd always been so much like two tomcats around one another that I never thought about where he'd come from, or what might have happened there. I didn't know what Terrance meant by things getting bad. But I could sure guess at it. Maybe he had his own cottonwood somewhere back east. And whatever had happened had made his ma run and his pa turn stranger.

I wondered if Ma had thought of running after Little Si died. Of just quitting everything and starting over again. Or if Pa had thought of running. Probably would've been easier to go on the road alone, not dragging a woman and two girls with him. Maybe running was a heck of a lot easier than trying to fix something so far broke it didn't seem it would ever go right again. I looked at Terrance with the words beating against his chest and fighting their way out. And I knew that no matter what, some of those words would never come. He'd carry some inside him forever, maybe. Or maybe I wasn't the right person to spill them to. It was like he was scared. Scared of breaking and having someone see it. Scared of what else might fall apart. I realized that even with everything that had happened to me, losing the farm, losing Little Si, sleeping under the stars, I never doubted that we'd stick together. Even back in Texas, with Pa so angry about that broken windshield. Some part of me knew that the worst had happened and we were still standing, me,

Pa, Ma, and Jess. And we were standing together.

It *was* different for me. But not for the reason Terrance thought. He had stopped talking, staring off to the side like he thought maybe I had words coming that might try to break him apart just a little bit more than he already was. But I didn't. For the first time I didn't want to boast, chide, or bet. I wanted to do something with my words, I wanted to say something honest and strange and hard to get quite right.

"What's your ma's name?" I asked.

For a moment, I thought he wouldn't answer me, or he'd bark back something mean about leaving things be. But he just kept staring off to the side until a word bubbled up.

"Joanna," he said.

The name changed his face and a little bit of softness crept in at the corner of his eyes. Like he was tasting something sweet. And then—

"I'm sorry for what I said about your pa, and I'm sorry I shoved you, and I'm real sorry I laughed at you . . . mostly, I just . . . if we strike, chances are we won't get another chance to play the apricot boys and I . . . darnit, I just want to wipe that smirk off Arlon's face."

The room changed color, warm and glowing. "Terrance, I wanna send that smirk to kingdom come!"

He looked at me, eyes lively. "Gloria, I wanna see Arlon walk on home with his tail between his legs!"

"Terrance, I want everyone at the apricot orchard to know Arlon got beat!"

"I wanna see the look on his face when we—"

"—when we show up—"

"I wanna get word out—"

"I say we do it—"

"Organize a game—"

"It's gotta be soon—"

"Tomorrow, otherwise who knows who'll be here—"

"Well, we gotta get word out—"

"I'll send Quentin—"

"Wait!" I put my hand up, grinning. "We gotta send Jess. She's got someone to see over there." If Joe Franklin's sweet son was just a mile away with his pockets full of apricots, then Jess would find him. And she wasn't too far gone that she'd forget to do our important business in the meantime. Besides, she could make her way through a sea of clipboard men better than anyone I knew.

She, as Quentin would say, was good as gold.

"All right, Gloria," said Terrance, "all the same, let's get Quentin to round up the team. We can fit in one more game, no matter if there's a strike or not. And ah . . . I gotcha pretty good, huh?"

I touched my bruising cheek and clicked my tongue. "You oughtta see the other guy."

"Glo?" asked Terrance.

"Yeah?"

He held out his hand. "From now on, you and I are playing for the same team, right?"

The air was alive, and when I shook his hand it crackled and sparked.

"Right."

We swung open the door to Terrance's little shanty expecting to go find Quentin. But he was already there. And so was Clyde, and the rest of the team, like they'd watched me walk in and had been waiting to see what we'd make of our tussle. And there was Jess, and a crowd of kids coming to see what the hubbub was all about. Seemed like everyone in the camp was there, except Davey of course.

Terrance and I stood, unsure of exactly what to do or say. But everyone was waiting like they were sitting in the pew and we were standing at the pulpit.

There was nothing else to do but speak.

"Listen up," Terrance said, "and listen close before this meeting gets called a meeting and busted up."

The kids nodded and leaned in.

"Seems like strike's on everyone's mind."

They rustled and hummed.

"Seems like we all might be gone tomorrow, or half of us gone, but whatever happens, it ain't gonna be the same. So before we go, we gonna challenge the boys from the apricot team to one last game. Ain't that right, Glo?"

All the eyes darted at me like a thousand little flames. More people looking at me than had ever looked at me before in my life. More people listening to me than had ever listened to me before in my life. Even Jess was tuned in.

"That's right, Terrance. We got one more chance to beat 'em. We got a, a person who's gonna go . . . talk to them—"

"Emissary!" whispered Quentin.

"That's right, we got an emissary gonna go get word to the apricot boys and set it up. And then, tomorrow, we gonna play one last time. And . . . and y'all oughtta come out, cheer us on, 'cause we playing for the peach orchard!"

A little cheer went up that promised more if I gave them more.

"Y'all oughtta come out 'cause we playing for better wages!"

The cheer was coming from bellies now, full-throated and rich.

"Y'all oughtta come out, 'cause we playing this last game for *Davey*!"

And the cheer burst out like a river you can't keep dammed up. I thought for sure the clipboard men would be coming now, even if we were just kids.

"But hey!" cried a voice. "How we gonna get there? Front gate's locked!"

I turned to Terrance, grinning like a cat with a bowl full of cream.

"Who said you getting there by way of the front gate?"

Chapter Twenty-One

When Pa came in that evening, he stood for a moment at the door, late sun blasting gold behind him. Ma stopped fussing with the pan and looked at him. He nodded once and even I knew what that meant.

The strike was happening.

"Pack your things," said Pa. "We gotta be ready to move tomorrow."

Jess and I packed what little we had into boxes. Everything but our mattress and pillows. Still, I pulled my Texas baseball out, wrapped it in a kerchief, and nestled it down between Ma's pots and pans in the powdered milk box. I figured if anything was going to get to the next destination safely it was Ma's skillets. When Jess was nearly finished packing, she took her little coffee tin of starlet cutouts and pulled off the top. I watched her out of the corner of my eye as she pulled them out one by one and laid them on the floor. Jean Harlow in a dress Ma said was "not decent," Myrna Loy leaning back like she was about to get kissed, and even that sad lady who threw herself off the Hollywood sign.

I eyed her from the other side of our mattress, waiting to see if she would pull the little stack of leaflets out that she'd squirreled away. But when I heard the *ping* of her nails hit the bottom of the tin, my head popped up.

"What?" she asked.

I crawled over on my knees and pried the coffee tin from her hands.

Empty.

"Where'd you . . . I mean, what'd you . . ."

Her face was still water and calm sky.

"Don't know what you mean, Glo," she said.

"Doggonnit, did you . . . You gone *Red*, Jess?" I whispered.

"What a thing to say," she said as she collected the silver cutouts. "Now if you'll excuse me, I got some *emissary* work to do."

She popped the lid back on the tin and placed it

carefully on top of Pa's toolbox and sauntered out.

"Where you off to?" called Pa.

She shrugged. "Ain't I got a right to take a stroll?"

Pa blinked. "Just don't stir anything up. You be back here by eight, hear?"

She nodded and let the door bang behind her. I popped open the lid of the coffee tin just to make sure my stack of contraband really was gone. It was. Either Jess had tossed them down an outhouse, or burned them up in the cookstove, or . . .

Pa snapped his fingers at me.

"You," he said, "let's go."

Oh, brother.

I stood up like a man on his way to the gallows. Pa opened the door into the molten evening sunlight. Blinding as it was, I stepped out into the warm air, into the electric hum of something stirring, and into the realization that this was probably the last time I'd be looking down these rows of shanties.

And that was just fine. I was part cowboy anyway. And cowboys sleep under the stars and cook on open fires and aren't bothered by not knowing what tomorrow brings. Still, I wasn't sure what a cowboy did when he disappointed his pa. Hadn't seen that in a picture yet.

Pa walked next to me, hands in his pockets, his

steps easy and long. We came to the end of a row of shanties where we could see a stretch of California pine and blue mountains beyond on the other side of the chain link.

"Sit," Pa said.

I sat, pulling my knees up and fixing my eyes on a great purple ridge miles away.

"Ma says you been ducking work."

I stared harder at the mountain, watching a tiny black speck of a hawk moving slowly in the distance.

"Ma says you've been playing baseball instead."

"I'm the pitcher," I said, looking at the toes of my boots.

"No doubt," said Pa.

Pretty soon his words would come. Words about not letting him and Ma down, about how they had too much on their minds already. About how having a wild child like me was just a little more than they could handle. And I wanted to save him the trouble of saying all that. I wanted to do the right thing. To say the hardest thing so he didn't have to say something he'd said so many time before.

"I'm sorry, Pa," I said.

Underneath me I felt the earth soften, like it was going to swallow me up.

"I'm sorry I keep getting out of line. I'm sorry I'm not the kind of kid that makes it easy for their ma and pa. I'm sorry I keep giving you reasons to be ashamed of me—"

Pa's eyes shot straight into mine.

"Ashamed of you?"

"Yeah. And I'm sorry you keep having to give me a talking-to, I know you got other things on your mind and I—know I'm not like Jess. I know it'd be easier if I were like Jess."

Pa let his head drop to his chest and then picked it back up to look out over the mountains. He was looking for answers in them, just like me.

"Glo," Pa said, "I don't want you to be like Jess any more than I want Jess to be like you."

I watched as another hawk joined the first one in the sky.

"You're my kid, that's all I want you to be. . . . I'll try to be better at reminding you of that."

He sat back a little and pulled his hat off his head. The top two buttons of his shirt were undone and there was a sheen of sweat across his collarbone. A slick lock of hair fell loose across his face. I watched him crumple the rim of his hat in his hand and I knew I needed to say one more thing.

"There's something else," I said.

Pa flipped his hat over in his hands. "So spill it."

"It was me who told Davey to get up that ladder. I wanted to practice my whips, so I told him to finish up for me, 'cause I knew he would. If I hadn't've done that, he'd be walking around and not lying half dead."

It was an awful thing to say out loud. So awful, Pa was quiet. And then he breathed in long and slow, closing his eyes.

"Gloria Mae," he said. "I need you to promise me something."

I nodded. My voice was broken and down the well of my throat, swimming somewhere in my stomach.

"Davey fell because he was on a piece of farm equipment that shouldn't've been out. No one should've been on it. Not even a kid as small as Davey. Don't you dare take his fall on your back."

The hawks beyond were making wide arcs through the sky.

"Promise me," he said slowly, "you will never, ever, *ever*, hold yourself responsible for what happens when grown folk do something wrong or just plain stupid."

I wasn't exactly sure what he meant, or how to tell when it was a grown folk and not me that made a mess of things. But I understood one thing, that he was telling me Davey's fall wasn't my fault. So I held out my hand so we could shake on it, since my voice was still climbing out of my stomach. After we shook, we sat there for a while. I'd said my piece, but there was something more hanging in the air. Some unfinished business.

"Sometimes I'm so damn mad at the world, Gloria," Pa said.

I guess that was it. I guess I could've said *Me too*, but I was pretty sure Pa knew that.

"Listen, Glo," he said, "tomorrow's not gonna be easy. Round midday, I want you off the orchard, you hear?"

"Is that when the strike's happening?"

Pa snapped his head up at me. "Listen, nothing's happening at all if the bosses know when it's coming. You understand? Word gets out when we're walking and the police'll be ready before we even start. That'll spook everyone. There's already too many folks who are skittish. Too many folks who could go either way."

I nodded.

"Don't nod at me, tell me you understand."

It was the first time Pa had told me anything about what was going on. Even though he wasn't telling me exactly what was going on.

"I understand, Pa," I said.

But it was one thing to organize a baseball game. It was another thing to try to turn the tide against folks that had coppers on their side. I thought of

Jimmy's pa getting beat and of the sound the billy club had made against Grady's head.

"Pa?" I asked.

"Yeah, Gloria?"

"Are there enough of us?"

"What do you mean?"

"I mean . . . supposing we walk out . . . are there enough of us?"

Pa's hand tightened around his hat. "I hope so, Gloria."

I thought of Grady and the leaflets under his floorboards. Some of them had been marked *Michelson's*. He must've been planning something before he got kicked out. Something big. Arlon had said the orchard was made of dynamite. All it needed was a match.

"What about the apricot orchard?" I said. "Ain't they in the same way?"

Pa looked at his hands. "Sure."

"So can't we just walk out at the same time?"

Pa glanced at me. "Well . . . ," he said slowly, "yeah, it'd be better with more. Mr. Blight thinks so, and I do, too. But we can't exactly saunter over to Michelson's and just ask around for whoever's in charge of planning a walkout over there. We gotta do this alone. It's not ideal, but sometimes you just need to get your little corner of the world right."

Wheels were turning in my brain.

All it needs is a match . . .

"You hear me?" said Pa.

"I hear ya."

"Good. Now listen, I want you and your sister off the orchard by midday."

I twisted my feet under me. "Well, as it happens, we got a game against the apricot boys."

Pa nodded. "Good. You taking Jess?"

"Couldn't keep her away with wild horses."

Pa looked to the mountain again. "You taking some of the other kids?"

"Pa, that's sort of top secret—"

"You taking some of the other kids?"

"Yessir."

"Good . . . Listen, if it goes well, we'll be outside the main gate after your game. You come meet us there. Me and your ma will be waiting for you."

"Okay," I said.

Pa stood up quickly. I guess there was nothing more to tell. He held his hand out to me. I took it, and he hoisted me up.

"Let's get on back," he said.

As we walked back to our shanty I noticed the world had gone from gold to blue. I'd been walking with my head down before, but now I was looking everywhere, and out of every window I could see eyes peeping out, glinting and winking with the rising moonlight. Watching and waiting and ready.

When we were almost at our door, Pa started chuckling.

"What's so funny?" I asked.

"I *was* taking you out here to give you a talking-to, ducking work and slugging boys. *Lord*."

He clicked his tongue. "Gloria Mae Willard, you're as wild as I was."

If he was trying to chide me, it wasn't working. It was more like he'd fixed a medal on my shoulder.

"So why'd you change your mind?" I asked, hoping it was dark enough to cover up my grin.

"Because I couldn't bear you thinking I'm ashamed you're my daughter. Lordy, Gloria, if I got half the courage you do, we just might pull this off tomorrow, apricot orchard or no."

All the stars in the sky twinkled on at the same time.

At our door, Pa put his hand on the knob and paused. He turned towards me and even though it was dark, his face was free of worry for the first time since I could remember. It was calm and gentle and good. We could've been standing on the porch back in Oklahoma in a field full of green with a full Sunday dinner cooking inside. We could've been coming back from town with a package of sugar for Ma and a

glamour magazine for Jess. We could've been thinking that everything would be easy and fine, even
when it was hard, for the rest of our days.

"Gloria," he said, "I hope you win tomorrow."

I beamed up at him. "I hope you do, too."

He ducked into the dark cabin just as Jess sauntered up right behind me. From the smudge of dirt
on the front of her dress and the glow on her face I
could tell that she'd finally found who she was looking for on the other side of the fence.

"You got the word out?" I asked. "About
tomorrow's game?"

"Among other things," she said.

"Well, you and I got one more piece of business
to take care of this evening."

Jess grinned. "Oh? And what's that?"

"We got a pickup to make."

"A pickup?"

"Yeah. There're some matches under the floorboards in seventy-two I think the apricot boys could
use."

Chapter Twenty-Two

When the morning alarm bell went off at day-break the next day, it was almost loud enough to drown out the whispering.

I could hear it coming through the thin walls of the shanty. I could hear it even when Jess shouted for Ma and Pa to walk on ahead of us and we wouldn't be too far behind. And it seemed to get louder as she stuffed every pocket of my overalls full of the rest of Grady's leaflets, which we'd smuggled out of his cabin the night before. By the time she was done, I looked as thick as a circus strong man. All I needed was a mustache and a barbell.

As we stepped out into the dazzling white light of morning, the whispers became a chorus. You could feel it everywhere. It was surging through our feet and coming off porches like a church song. But best of all, it was in the faces of folks as they walked through to the orchard. Like we were all in it together. Like we could be bigger than anything or anyone. Like we were more than lost land and dirty clothes and trucks with bad brakes and cracked windshields.

As we walked I poked her in the side.

"Was it you putting the leaflets in the sorting house and on the clotheslines and all that?"

Jess was holding her head high and acting holier-than-thou, like she was on her way to church. "I ain't no rabble-rouser, Glo. I got better things to do with my time than pass out things no one's gonna read."

Seemed like a funny thing to say given that I was packed to the gills with things we were betting people would read.

Still, there was the faintest little hint of satisfaction at the edge of her lips.

Up ahead of us, Pa was walking tall. Might as well have been riding a trusty steed, reins in one hand with the sun glinting off silver spurs. Next to him, I saw Sam Blight walking with his wife, who was holding their little baby. For once it didn't bother me.

All around us, word was passing from kid to kid. When to duck, where to go, what to do if a man with a clipboard saw you sneaking out. But I was pretty sure no men with clipboards were worried about a couple kids sneaking off. Not when all the grown folk were thick as thieves and ready to walk, leaving all those peaches hanging up in the air.

When it was time to split, we made it to the fence in no time, and I shimmied under it and then pulled the chain link back with all my might to keep Jess's dress from getting too mussed up. She'd slept with her hair in pin curls the night before and not even a gown fit for one of her starlet ladies could've made her look prettier, gingham and all. She had the extra bit of brightness that you can't get with a hair curl, or a bit of rouge or even a high-heeled shoe. And I knew why. And she knew why. And she didn't mind me knowing. And that made me feel almost grand.

Clyde was already on the other side of the fence, and he waited for us to catch up. Behind us we heard the whispering of the littler ones looking for the hole, finding it, and shooting under it like prairie dogs. And as we walked through the tall grasses, the green came alive with the rushing of kids from the orchard. Some of them were walking alongside us, some were scrambling to catch up. Everyone looked pleased as punch to not be halfway up a tree picking peaches you couldn't even eat.

Our little baseball field was almost the color of springtime after a good long rain. Open and wide and edged with the long rushes and reeds, wildflowers peeping in to get a piece of the action. It was all kinds of beautiful, even the critters scurrying through the brush were saying so in their chitters and chirps.

First person I saw was Joe Franklin's sweet son. He was standing with his hands in his pockets. His face flashed happy when he saw me, but it was Jess he was looking for. She walked right up and held out her hand for his, like he owed it to her. And he paid up right away.

"What took you so long?" he said, smiling like a summer afternoon.

Jess glanced coyly at the ends of her fingers. "Who says I been looking for you?"

He grinned and took his cap off with his free hand.

"Hello, Ben," I said, thinking I could still call him Joe Franklin's sweet son in my mind.

"Well, hi there, Gloria," he said, and stepped back so I could see the rest of the field.

And standing in the middle, arms crossed like

they'd been waiting on us, were the apricot orchard boys. And behind them, gads of littler ones, sitting scrawny and big-kneed on the cool ground.

We stopped and stared.

Arlon turned and smiled his blue-ribbon smile.

"Jessamyn said you was bringing the camp. So we brought ours, too. Ain't gonna let you get all the cheers. Wouldn't be fair."

All this time I'd been so glad just to play I hadn't thought about having a crowd to watch us, yelling and cheering. Now, I could almost imagine the smell of peanuts and hot dogs. When this strike was over maybe we'd set up somewhere else. All of us. Me, Clyde, Terrance, Quentin, even Arlon and Joe Franklin's sweet son. And maybe we'd keep on playing with a basket of ham sandwiches waiting on the side and a pitcher of punch. Maybe there'd be Sundays off every week and maybe Pa'd build benches for the old folk to sit on and maybe Jess and Joe Franklin's sweet son would sit elbow to elbow and act like they weren't jumpy as grasshoppers. Maybe Pa'd call us over before we started and say something to get our hopes up and maybe he'd turn to the other pas and say, "That girl over there? Only girl on the team? That's my girl."

I'd lose a hundred times to Arlon Mackie and the others if it meant we could keep going.

"Little bird told me peach orchard's walking out today," Arlon said.

Speak of the devil.

"Little bird told me the same thing," I said.

Every set of eyes, from every corner of each orchard, was looking at me.

"Terrance tells me it's your pa who got the whole thing going again."

I nodded, remembering Grady and the club at the back of his skull. The memory of the sound of it shocked through me and for a moment I thought of Pa picking his teeth up from the floor of a jail cell like Jimmy's dad might've done. But Pa wasn't alone. Pa would have everyone with him. I found Arlon's eyes again.

"That's right," I said.

"Well, you tell your pa, Gloria," he said, "if the peach orchard goes, apricot's gonna follow. Right now, we're all just waiting for a reason."

Jess cleared her throat behind me.

I reached into my pockets and pulled out the tight little stacks of leaflets. Arlon took one from me and thumbed through it. He gave a long whistle and cocked his head. Behind him, a kid came up, scorched and sun-weathered with teeth somehow blinding white. "Maybe y'all just need a little push," I said.

"You got more?" Arlon said as the kid peered from behind.

I nodded and reached into my back pockets for the rest of them.

Arlon turned to the sun-scorched kid. "Take these and put 'em somewhere safe."

The kid nodded, pocketed the leaflets, and slipped away.

I guess that was that.

Arlon stepped back, spreading his arms out wide like a ringmaster. "Well then, y'all ready to get beat one last time before this whole place blows?"

The apricot kids let up a whoop and a holler.

I was grinning now. "Only thing that's gonna blow this place wide open is the look on your face when I strike you out."

This time the whooping and hollering was coming from behind me.

I was grinning.

Arlon was grinning.

"Play ball!" Quentin cried, and we scattered to our places like we'd been itching to get there all our lives.

Chapter Twenty-Three

The peach orchard side of the crowd was going wild, whistling and cheering and waving.

Clyde picked up the bat and swung it over his shoulder. He had to hit this one good or we were done for. It was 2–1 with the apricot boys in the lead and this was our last chance to score. By some stroke of luck, I'd hit the ball and made it all the way to first, but not before the apricot boys got a second out. Terrance was on third base, ready to run. If Clyde hit this one good, even if only me and Terrance made it home, we'd be one run up on them. Then all we had to do was hold the score. Terrance and me locked eyes and then we turned towards Clyde, nodding and shouting *You can do it* without even opening our mouths. We didn't have to, because all the peach orchard kids were shouting it loud and clear.

Quentin and the rest of our team were on their feet ready to jump and cheer or yell and throw their caps in the dirt depending on what happened. If we didn't score, the game was over. We knew it, they knew it, and the crowd knew it. The camp kids were sitting and clapping and hollering from their grassy seats, half of them hoping we'd make it and half of them hoping we wouldn't.

The apricot pitcher wound his ball back and—

A swing and a miss.

Thunk.

"Come on, Clyde," I said under my breath.

The ball shot back to the pitcher and he wound it back again, sent it flying, and—

Another swing and a miss.

Thunk.

Our side was getting quiet. Leaning in like if they just kept still, the bat would meet the ball. The other side was getting louder and more excited.

"Come on, Clyde," I heard Terrance say.

My hands were gripping my knees and my eyes were staring so hard Clyde must've felt them. Because he looked up just then and—

And he *smiled*. He winked, so fast only I could

see it, and hoisted the bat up over his shoulder. I started grinning because I could see now Clyde was playing with them. Making them think he was tired by missing. Clyde was our best batter—if he couldn't do it, no one could. I bounced on my knees because we were gonna have to run soon.

The pitcher wound back, let her fly, and—

SMACK!

That ball flew high and long up into the sky!

I started running like my tail was on fire. I let the hum-thrush of the crowd whooping carry me past second base—tin can lid—past third base—pried-off side of a fruit box—and Terrance was home! And I was blazing up quick behind.

Thwack! Someone had thrown the ball to someone behind me—just a few more steps and I'd be home safe, my feet were starting fires in the dust because I could feel one of them apricot boys winding up his arm to sling it forward and—

SHASHHHHH! Red grating fire burned up my whole side as I slid in the dirt and a flash of earthy dust and I was *home!*

"Safe!"

Thwack! went the ball into the catcher's glove above me and *thwack* it went as it sailed through the sky and into the hands of the second baseman, who easily tagged Clyde out.

That was three. Three outs and we were at the bottom of the last inning with the apricot boys batting. The whole field shifted as we changed positions. The apricot boys, who thought they were gonna go home with another win, now had one last inning to make that happen.

We were in the lead now, 3–2, and all we had to do was keep them from scoring. What felt like a sure loss a moment ago was now buzzing and whispering possibilities. We were thinking it, the peach orchard kids were thinking it, and best of all, the apricot boys were thinking it.

The crowd was going wild like we were at a rodeo, not a patch of trampled-down ground turned into a baseball field. I saw Jess nestled in the crook of Joe Franklin's sweet son's arms. She looked just right there and so did he. Hadn't thought it would matter, but seeing someone from back home made me want to win all the more, even if he was an apricot boy, technically speaking.

As the dust settled around me I turned from Jess to the other peach orchard kids, to the apricot kids. You'd almost think we were home somewhere, that we all knew each other. That we all saw each other and our families in the fields every day, or sat behind one another at church, or elbowed each other in school. That this kid wasn't from Arkansas and this one from Nebraska and this one from Colorado. Right now we were all just orchard kids.

Quentin pulled me up and Terrance clapped his arm around my shoulders. The three of us rushed in to the rest of the team and huddled around one another.

"This is it," Terrance said. "We hold 'em or we lose."

We all nodded. And no one was saying it, but it came down to me. I was standing between us and the win. And no one said it, but once we broke out of this huddle, I'd be up on the mound alone, by myself, hoping and praying I could hold 'em back.

"You got to hold 'em off, Gloria," Casey said. "You're our first line of defense. But if they do hit, we right behind you."

I nodded. I wasn't scared of striking any of them out, or of the rest of the team being able to catch the ball and send it back. But Arlon had a swing like no one else did on either team. And they were saving him for last. They'd set their lineup so he could clean up when the bases were loaded, when it was time. Then all he had to do was knock it into the tall grasses beyond our reach, and the game would be over.

I wasn't going in blind this time. I knew what I was up against. And I knew that if I said I was scared out loud, whatever chance I had would vanish. I looked around our little huddle from eye to eye. We were close, so close. You could hear the wanting of winning whispering around us. It was itching the tips of our fingers.

And I wanted to win. I did. I wanted to be the reason we won. But there was something I wanted more.

To stay. To be here, belonging with this ragtag group of players that dug holes under fences. That kept showing up even when they lost. That timed escapes to *Dick Tracy* and the sound of a machine-gun-loud engine. That threw stones up to me in the trees. That let little bits of their truth bubble up and out so I could see them, raw and bent and almost broken, but not. I wanted to be here forever, even more than our farmhouse. Even more than the stunted wheat fields back in Oklahoma. Even more than I wanted to be sitting under Si's cottonwood, and sometimes I wanted to sit there real bad.

My dreaming dropped as the team let up a whoop and went scattering to their places, Terrance in the outfield, Quentin behind the batter's mound, Clyde on first. The cheering of the crowd felt ten times bigger. I walked slow to the pitcher's mound, reached it, and turned to see who they were sending me.

It was a little guy about my height, wincing into

the sun and setting his jaw like he was four times older.

I nodded to Quentin, crouching behind him.

He nodded back.

I pulled the ball up to my shoulder, looking down the bridge of my nose from me to him.

I wound the ball up over my head and sent it flying fast down the path I set it on.

Thunk!

"Strike one!"

The little guy chewed the inside of his cheek and settled back into his readiness.

Quentin's sure arm sent the ball back and I caught it like I was picking a peach out of the air.

And *thunk!*

Strike two.

And back to me.

The little guy's eyes had hardened into steel and his whole body was tense with the thought of losing. He wanted to hit the ball as much as I wanted him to miss.

"Sorry, pal," I said under my breath, and—

Thunk!

Strike three.

One out.

The peach kids cheered and the next guy was just as easy. He came up quaking a little, and seemed almost glad by the third strike that it was over.

Two outs.

Something had happened on the apricot boys'
side. They had gathered and were talking in hushed
voices. Once in a while one of them popped his head
up like a groundhog and looked my way.

I turned to Terrance. His look said *Hold steady.*

I turned to Quentin. His look said *Breathe.*

I turned to Clyde. He was tying his shoe.

Well then.

The apricot boys scattered and a lean boy in blue
came up to the plate, tapping it once or twice with
the tip of his bat like he was knocking on wood.

"Lordy," I said under my breath. They were
gonna bring everything they had, I could feel it. It
was humming in the wind and tickling the earth like
an underground spring.

"Don't break, girl," I said low. It was the closest
I'd been to praying since Oklahoma.

The boy in blue swung the bat up over his shoulder, muscles flexing down his arm.

He meant business.

But so did I.

I wound the ball up, sending another prayer into
my right arm, and snapped my wrist so it would
curve nasty.

Thunk!

One down.

"Don't break, girl," I whispered.

Quentin sent the ball back to me, straight and true, I caught it in my right hand and rubbed it against my overalls like to make it shine.

I wound it up like a preacher's words and—

Thunk!

Two down.

The boy in blue spat, looked down to the ground, and turned back to his team, flicking some kind of sign at them with his thumb and his pinky.

They signed back with their pointer fingers circling the air like vultures.

Well, darnit. Heck if I knew what they were talking about.

The boy swung the bat up once more.

I could give it to him straight after sending him curve balls, or I could send him a curve ball because maybe he was thinking I'd send it to him straight.

Shoot.

"Well, here goes nothing," I murmured, wound it back, and sent it spinning.

THWACK!

Out over the field it went, as high as the hollers from the apricot kids! Danny was running for it, but even I could see he wouldn't get there before it bounced, to get the boy in blue out. It bounced once right into his hands and he threw the ball hard to Clyde, but it was too late. The boy in blue had gotten to first base, fair and square.

It put some wind in the apricot boys' sails.

But we still had it. We still had the lead. First base wasn't a run. Not even close.

The next batter came up to the plate, thick-armed and grinning.

Aw, shoot.

He chewed on whatever cud was in his mouth and spat black into the dirt.

"Hold steady, Glo," I whispered.

He missed the first pitch.

But he got the second.

It was a scutter ball, rolling and bouncing like a tumbleweed, kicking up dirt like a pony. The boy in blue was on second. The thick-armed cud chewer was on first.

And the ball was back in our hands.

"Aw, Lordy," I said.

Second and first. Just where Terrance and I had been the inning before.

"Aw, Lord," I said.

Arlon Mackie was coming up. White-toothed like a film star, with a swagger to match. He was coming up and it sent the apricot orchard side of the field into a frenzy.

Because they knew. They knew this was it. They knew Arlon was gonna bring it home.

He walked up to the plate, slinging the bat, which weighed nothing in his arms. It was made of air, or dynamite, or something in between.

He was coming up to the plate. Coming up to send us to kingdom come.

"Hey, Glo!" I heard.

Jess had wriggled out of Joe Franklin's sweet son's arms and was running towards me.

I squinted to see her with the blinding sunlight around her like she'd gone holy on me.

"Catch!" she said, and tossed something white-brown and ruddy through the air.

It was my Texas baseball, flying towards me like a summer swallow. She must have fetched it when I wasn't looking. Dropped it in the wide pocket of her apron and let it bounce against the side of her calf with each step.

It landed in my hands like it was made to be there. I looked down on it. Ruddy and mud-colored, beat and batted at. Almost as dirty as my fingernails. Covered in Oklahoma, Texas, New Mexico, Arizona, and now California. Covered in every place I'd been. Knowing every time I'd ever thrown it. Knowing everything I wanted. Knowing me.

I dropped the other ball in the dirt.

"Watchu playing at?" called an apricot boy.

"Switching out balls," I said.

"You cheating? Give it here."

I tossed it his way. The apricot boy turned it over in his hand and looked back at the rest of his team.

"Just a baseball," he called.

He would say that. He tossed it back to me and I caught it, warm and ready.

The sun was beating down and sending a glimmer up between where I stood and where Arlon was. His bat was waggling back and forth, slow and deliberate. My hands gripped the leather of the ball, the little bits of grit pressing into the pads of my fingers, my thumb running over the stitching. Hundreds of little red loops holding the whole thing together.

Last time he'd hit it on the first try. This time I had to hold him off three times.

Three times.

How do you hold off the best batter anyone's got three times?

I loved my right arm, loved it fierce, but it was gonna take more than bone and muscle to keep the apricot boys from winning.

I closed my eyes and saw the farmhouse. Blue steps leading up to the front door. Cellar full of canned beans. Crack running down my wall. Rosalita and Yvonne pecking at the dirt in the back.

Breathe.

I took the farmhouse up into my hand. Gathered it up, felt the weight of it in my hand, its chipped paint, Ma's wedding curtains, Pa's tools, wound it back, sent it flying, and—

Thunk!

Quentin had the ball and Arlon was blinking into the sun like the rug got pulled out from underneath him.

He'd missed.

One time. Twice more and we'd win.

"Come on back," I said low.

Quentin sent the ball in an arc through the sky like he could hear me asking for it.

Arlon took a practice swing that sliced through the air. And hoisted the bat up again.

Breathe.

I gathered up that night. That night when Ma screamed and brought a little baby into the world and I was afraid to touch him but I did and he was warm as fresh bread and louder than a freight train. I took it into my hand, all that wonder, like me and the whole earth knew the same secret, and felt it grow hot in my fingers and—

Thunk!

Arlon near spun around with all that swing missing all that ball.

He cussed. Loudly.

Two down. One more strike to get him out. One more strike. One more fastball, curve ball, any ball. I didn't need to look back to the team to know they were rooting for me. I felt it in the air. I felt it in the trees shaking their leaves back and forth above. I felt it in the shutterbugs down in the earth, in the field mice scurrying in the grasses. I felt it beating from the peach orchard kids, who had crept closer just to see if all this was real. I felt it coming from Jess.

Maybe it was luck, those first two. Might've been. Sometimes you get lucky, everyone knew that. Maybe those two strikes were nothing but God cutting me some slack after a hard run.

Arlon was biting down hard and giving me a stare like he meant business.

Now or never.

I listened for a moment. Listened to the whir of the crowd. Listened to them sending my name up to the sky like hope. Listened to the shuffling back and forth of the apricot boys, who couldn't stand still knowing they were so close to losing. Listened to all the fists of the peach orchard kids tearing up grass to keep from running wild with excitement. Some of them even looked like they was praying.

I thought of Pa speaking up for the peach orchard. Speaking up for Davey. I thought of our little shanty. I thought of the strike, I thought of leaving.

"Breathe, Glo," I murmured.

I thought of being on the road, I thought of knocking on doors. I thought of me going to some asparagus farm and Quentin heading to pull carrots somewhere else and Terrance going south for the orange crop.

"Breathe, Glo."

I pulled everything I had up into my right arm, wound it back, and shot everything I had through my fingertips and—

SMACK!

The sound was sick and awful.

And I took every ounce of everything I had left in me and launched myself to the right, arms outstretched for something, anything. I heard the hollering. I saw them leaping to their feet. But I was airborne, flying, nothing under me but space and losing again. It hit me like a punch in the gut, nearly turning my lungs inside out.

I landed hard, my shoulder scraping along the dirt and my knees coming instinctively up to my chest. I felt the gravel grind into my skin as dirt filled my mouth and eyes. In one breath I had breathed it in deep, the California dust. A ringing buzzed into my ears and behind it was half screaming and half moaning.

I didn't have to look to know that behind me the apricot boys were running around the bases. No doubt the ball was somewhere in the grasses beyond, or sailing through the clouds, or burning up in the heat of the sun.

I opened my eyes to see the bright blue California sky.

Above, a bird sailed miles up.

Quentin popped his head into my view.

"Gloria? You okay?"

The ringing was fading. His face was coming into focus.

"Sure thing, boss," I said.

Then there was Danny. And Casey. And Pete and Holden, too. And finally there was Terrance.

"You got it?"

I grinned.

"My pride?" I asked. "No siree."

Terrance rolled his eyes.

"The ball. You got the ball?"

Then there was an apricot boy. The little one with the jaw of a grandaddy.

"You catch it?"

I was curled up tightly around something like I was keeping it safe.

"Let's see!" someone else said.

I felt broken but I unclenched myself and let my

limbs uncurl. There, between the flesh of my fore-arm and my belly, was the baseball.

I'd caught it.

"Golly . . . ," the boy with the grandaddy jaw breathed, and stepped back. "Y'all!" he called out. "Girl caught the ball, girl caught Arlon's ball!"

The team rushed around me, their voices making one big mess of joy and maybe a little disbelief.

Whatever run they'd scored while I'd been lying there didn't matter. Arlon had hit the ball but I'd caught it. With the buzzing and the dust clearing, I could've sworn I felt them lifting me up, up, up into the sky.

In some other life, there would've been a ticker-tape parade.

In some other place there would've been flashes and newspapermen.

Not that I cared.

This would be just fine.

All the boss men of all the orchards in all the world couldn't know how good this felt.

Chapter Twenty-Four

When the dust settled and the whooping wound down into a quiet sort of happiness, when the apricot boys had shaken our hands and when even Arlon had patted me on the back, when Jess found me grinning, half from watching me win and half from having listened to Joe Franklin's sweet son's heartbeat, I thought of Pa.

If it goes well, he'd said, *we'll be outside the main gate after your game.* His words dug at the bottom of my stomach like a stick in a pond, stirring up mud and leaving me unsettled.

One by one the apricot boys were tipping their

hats and slipping in through the tall grasses. The peach orchard kids had started to do the same, realizing someone might be missing them. I saw Joe Franklin's sweet son take Jess's fingertips and step back away while she glowed golden. Maybe his sweetness was contagious. Looking at Jess, it seemed like a fair amount had rubbed off on her.

Soon it was just us Willard sisters and the team.

The air was full of snaps and buzzes as we started moving back towards camp. Winning was shining off us like stardust, even in the bright midday sun. And though we were skipping down the road in clumps of twos and threes, there was something linking all of us. Like a flock of birds flying across prairie grass, or a group of minnows in a high summer stream.

Jess tugged my overall strap behind me and spun me around like a top. She was on the brink of saying something. She opened and closed her mouth a few times before she found the right words. "I just wanna say, Gloria, I'm awful proud to be your sister."

I stood and let her words fill me up until we were both grinning and giggling. We started running to catch up with the rest of the boys and the world blurred green and gold all around me. I heard it again and again: the smack of the ball, the hollering, the cheers of the peach kids. I saw it clearly as the road before me, Arlon's face when he shook my hand, not mocking, not angry, just real sportsman-like. If there was one thing I'd remember when I was old and gray, it'd be this. I'd hold on to this more than anything else.

Up ahead Terrance and Quentin had slowed. They peered back at the rest of us still laughing and dreaming ourselves back into the game we'd just won. But from the looks on their faces, they weren't dreaming at all. Something had brought them right back down to earth.

"What is it?" I called. "Why'd you stop?"

The rest of us slowed, too. All around us we could hear the lazy hot sounds of a summer after-noon. It was quiet, a little too quiet, not like what I thought a strike would sound like.

Didn't matter, we were still a ways off.

But the quiet of the world wasn't what was chill-ing the air now. Silence was spreading through the team as their laughs went up with the wind.

One by one, each boy that reached Terrance and Quentin looked down the road ahead, and then turned back to me and Jess with that same look on his face. Jess and I started running to join up with them and when we did, we got a clear view down the long, lonely road to the orchard. There was the big white gate we'd all come through, there was the chain link stretching out beyond. And there, lined up like black birds on a wire, were more police trucks than I could count.

The green and gold drained out of the world and our steps stopped skipping.

No one said anything. We stood and stared like if we looked hard enough those trucks would vanish. It was me who started walking again. And I heard everyone fall in line behind me.

I heard Rudy say, "Did it happen?"

Eugene said back, "Looks like it never got started."

Holden said, "Did someone tell?"

And then Casey said, "What do you know about it?"

Jess caught up with me and took my hand.

I kept staring at those cars. Looking into the back barred windows to see if there were any faces looking out. But they were as hollow as the inside of my chest.

A few policemen were standing against the trucks, making small talk and cracking jokes. They might've been hanging around outside of church, their ways were so easy. When they heard us, shuffling along like ghosts, they stopped and stared.

"Hey now," one of them called.

We kept walking.

"Hey, kiddos, don't know what you're looking for but it ain't here."

We kept going. The men didn't look angry, they didn't look scared. Just sort of bewildered. Like we'd walked out of a fog. We had tightened into a small little pod, bumping shoulders with one another.

One of the policemen went up and rapped on St. Peter's window. I saw St. Peter look up and throw his hands in the air. He came out waving away the policemen and saying, "Yeah, yeah, I know 'em, I know 'em. What you doing out? You looking for trouble?"

Quentin's bell-voice piped up, "No, sir, we're looking for—"

"Aw, never mind, get in! Get!"

St. Peter unlocked the gate and herded us in like sheep. As I passed by his little booth I looked inside. Inside was the man from the California Growers Association with the plum-colored silk across his hat. And standing next to him was Sam Blight. Chatting. Talking. I turned my head as we passed to see him get his hand shaken, to watch him get a slap on the back from the man who told us we shouldn't be asking for more. I felt Jess see him, too, because she bristled all at once. Her anger came off her like heat. But I was too confused to be angry. Seeing Mr. Blight talking to those men didn't make sense.

He was playing for us. He was on our team. He told me so.

Mr. Blight was laughing like the man with the plum-colored silk had told him the funniest joke he'd ever heard. His head arched back in a laugh that sent the smile on his mouth straight up into his eyes. But as his chin came down his eyes met mine and the color went from his face and his smile dropped like a stone. When he saw me, he looked almost scared of me. Normally it would have felt good. To have someone be just a little afraid of me. But somehow him knowing I'd seen him there made me want to blow away into a million seeds from a broke-open pod. It made me want to be a thousand tiny somethings that could flit on by without being anything to anyone.

I walked on. I could feel the eyes of the team on my back. Behind me, I heard a door open and a voice fumbling, "Gloria, hey! Hey, Gloria!" I turned and stopped, the rest of the team stopping with me.

Sam Blight had stumbled out through the door. His face was clouded over with something kind of like guilt.

"I'm sorry, kid," he said, "I'm real sorry."

Things were beginning to fall into their horrible place now.

"I gotta look after my own," he called, but I just kept walking.

The police trucks that looked like they'd been there for hours. Pa telling me the only way we had a chance was if the bosses didn't see it coming. Ma saying how odd it was that man with a baby would be so eager to lay everything on the line. Sam Blight sitting cozy with the man from the California Growers Association. Sam Blight apologizing to me. And the terrible empty silence that lined the shanties.

Jess's anger was lighting up mine now. It was coming off her in waves and it spread across my temples like a noon sun. That sad, sorry look on Blight's face made it burn hotter.

"Did he tell them about Pa? Did Mr. Blight tell them about the strike?" I whispered to Jess.

When she spoke it was like poison coming out of her mouth. "Don't you say his name," she said, "he ain't worth the dirt in my shoe."

We kept walking, me and Jess first and boys behind us. Somewhere off I heard one of the policemen crack another joke. Beyond the rows of shanties were the rows of trees, lightened of most of their load. And in those trees were men and women working like they always did. With their heads down like before. It was like Ma said. Being scared makes it harder to do the right thing. And someone had scared them real good from what I could see. Whatever was humming in the air that morning had gone up like the dew. Maybe it was the police cars. Maybe it was something the man from the California Growers Association had said. Maybe they made an example of Pa. Maybe he wasn't even here anymore.

I could see which one was our shanty all the way at the end of the line. There, lying out on the dirt, was all our stuff, like someone had gone through and thrown it out on purpose after we'd stacked it so nice and neat. There were Ma's cooking things lying like a pack of pick-up sticks. There was Jess's tin of starlets, open and blowing in the wind. Pa's clothes were scattered across the road, pants and overalls flattened and dirty. That old powdered milk crate we'd been using as a chair was split down the middle and someone had taken the sack of flour Ma paid too much for and opened it across our stuff. Our things were coated in white, and the glass jar of lard had been broken against a post and was melting into the earth. Two men were standing at the door smoking a cigarette, too caught up in whatever they were talking about to notice us.

And then I heard Pa's voice.

And I knew what was coming next.

I'd seen it before.

I heard it coming from down the road. Grown men's voices. Too many of them.

I heard Pa. Shouting back.

I thought of Old Man Grady at the gate.

I thought of what Terrance said about Jimmy's pa picking up his teeth.

I thought of all those policemen, and all those men in white.

I thought of all those pickers who should've been standing with my pa.

I thought of Sam Blight turning on us.

I thought of what they might have offered him: food, money. It didn't matter.

And when the pack of them came into view, like snarling dogs, chasing my pa, making him run, making him stumble, raising their hands, raising their billy clubs, that hot anger in me went full flame, full dynamite. It burned through my skin and in my eyes. It sent me running at them, earth light and crackling under my feet.

I ran towards the pack of them like a funnel cloud, like I was running to stop everything that ever took anything from me. I was running towards the dust that took Little Si, the bank man that took our farm. I was running towards every place that had turned us away, and every person that had called us something awful when they thought we weren't listening. I was running towards the Santa Ana Orchard and their bum wages and their bum ladders.

And I was screaming *No* like it was the only word in me.

It came hurtling out of my mouth like a war cry, or a peace cry, or just a cry. It brought the whirling world and my feet to a halt right in front of the man about to hit my pa and I locked my eyes on his and dug my feet into the earth like a tree that could stand tall whatever God sent its way.

The man froze like I was working magic on him.

He stumbled and blinked, his stick trembling up in the sky, looking small and insignificant against the incredible wide blue of the heavens.

Behind me I could hear Pa's astonished breath coming fast.

My own breath hissed out like steam.

And it took me a second of watching the man's eyes dart back and forth to finally realize I wasn't standing alone. Jess was to my right. Terrance to my left. Next to him was Clyde and standing next to Jess was Quentin. And there were Casey and Rudy, and everyone else standing together.

I'd been running towards the man with the club, but I hadn't been running alone. There were at least nine other souls that were as fed up as me with doing nothing. We were standing together, arms linked, not blinking or balking. We were fighting back without fighting. Standing for something just by standing in place. Holding on by holding together.

The policemen and the men in white stood there, not moving.

One of them said, "Go on!"

Another one said, "I ain't gonna hit a kid!"

And the next one said, "Just move 'em aside!"

They were unsure and skittish and I sent my voice barreling through them. It was louder than ten voices and stronger than my right arm could ever be. "Listen, y'all! I'm gonna tell you what's gonna happen. You gonna let me and my pa and my ma and my sister outta here with no trouble. You gonna let us take our stuff, and then you're gonna let us drive away. And I swear on the most beautiful cottonwood in all of Oklahoma that we will never come back here again."

My words hung in the air like gospel.

The man's stick dropped to his side. "You got ten minutes. And if I ever see you in this county again, you'll wish I'd thrown you in the clink in the first place."

The story came together in whispers as we packed up our things. Sam Blight had told the bosses about the strike before it happened. Probably got a raise to do it. Probably enough to take care of that wife and baby. By the time we were throwing the first pitch of the game the police trucks were lined up outside and along the fences where everyone could see. The man from the California Growers Association got up and said they had enough room at the jail to take half the camp, so folks were welcome to walk but they'd be walking right into the back of a squad car. Might've been enough, but Sam also told them it was Pa who was the leader and so they trashed our place and went looking for Pa, who'd already told Ma to go get the truck because we had to scram. And just about then they found Pa and chased him right into our path.

The team stayed by me as we picked up our things and put them back in order. The boys even helped Jess find most of her starlets. They helped load the truck when Ma brought it sputtering and popping up to 72. Then they walked with me to the gate to say goodbye.

Sometimes you need words and sometimes you got to ride off into the sunset. I wasn't sure what this particular situation called for, but I knew there wasn't much time before St. Peter kicked us off. I'd already pushed my luck, and no one wearing a white suit or holding a club was going to do me any more favors. The feeling of time slipping away made the air feel thick and wet. I looked at my team, at my friends. Even though the fruit was near picked, even though every one of them would be sent packing soon, I would've lost a thousand games against Arlon if it meant having a few more days with them.

"I guess this is so long," I said.

"Well," Quentin said, "we'll be right behind you, wherever you go next. Not many peaches left in those trees. Maybe it'll be cherries next. Or apples. Who knows?"

Clyde stepped forward and fished something out of his pocket. It was my baseball.

"You oughtta take it," he said. "I think it's lucky."

I pushed it back into his hands. "You give it to Davey when he wakes up. Tell him what he missed. Tell him he can give it back to me next we meet."

Clyde nodded and tucked the ball away. Behind him I caught Terrance's eyes. He wasn't the type to be verbose in a moment like this.

"Catch," he said softly, and tossed a golden-pink peach through the air. I caught it in my right hand, grinned, made sure St. Peter was looking at me, and bit right into it. It was warm and soft and sweeter than all the nectar in Eden.

And then I hopped up into the back, where Jess was sitting. She moved aside for me and I settled down next to her. As Ma revved the engine, I stood back up and spread my arms wide and said, "You gentlemen are good as gold. And I know I'll be seeing you soon."

The truck lurched forward, and Jess steadied me so I wouldn't lose my pride in front of my friends.

And even as they grew smaller and smaller I could feel every one of them believing what I'd said. It was too big a hope to get swallowed up by California pines, or a thousand miles of dusty road.

Epilogue

"Name?" said the man in the tan hat.

"Willard," said Pa.

The truck was bucking more than usual and I had to pee like a racehorse.

"How long you been in California?"

"Two months."

"You part of the trouble down at Michelson's?"

"Michelson's? Never heard of the place."

"Apricot grove. Went radical."

Next to me, Jess wound a lock of hair around her finger and I sat on my foot to keep from peeing.

"You don't say?"

"They might cave to Reds down there, but this neck of the woods ain't no place for rabble-rousers."

"Hear you loud and clear."

"How many you got?"

"Two grown and able-bodied, two young and able-bodied."

The man sighed and peeked in the back.

"Y'all like pears?" he said to me and Jess.

"Oh yessir," I said, "but just picking 'em, hate the taste."

The man gave me a look.

"Sure thing," he said. "No filching product."

I put my hand on my heart. "Not in a million years," I said.

He circled back around to the driver's side.

"Look, we got all we need, but I guess I can take you, being you're a family man."

"Much obliged," said Pa.

The man waved us through the gate of the Stockton Pear Orchard, shouting, "Cabin twenty-nine!"

We rolled in and Jess leaned out over the side of the truck. I grinned at her.

"I know who you're looking for," I said with a wink in my voice.

She waved her hand to brush me off and kept looking. Ever since we'd left she'd been writing letters to Joe Franklin's sweet son's granddad's place in Balko. "He'll get them one day," she had said when I caught her scribbling a note on the back of one of Pa's leaflets he kept tucked under the seat.

"What do you write to him?" I had asked.

She kept scribbling. "I tell him where we are and where we're going . . . and whatever I don't wanna say out loud."

I stood there letting her have her write until she blinked up at me. "Don't worry, Glo, you get most of the good bits." And then she picked up her pencil and kept at it.

Pa and Ma had found some folks at a government camp who were just as bent as we were about how things were going at places like the Santa Ana. But they'd also heard about Michelson's and said it went to show that a thousand people with nothing could beat a couple people with everything if they stuck together. They were headed up to the pear trees in the north and said that no matter what, we could at least travel together and keep an eye out for each other. When I asked Pa if they were radicals or Reds, or troublemakers, he just shrugged and said, "You should talk." When I asked Ma if we were gonna try striking under the pear trees, instead of hushing me up she just said, "We gonna do what's right, this time, every time, from now on."

We rolled up in front of 29 and I jumped up and out as fast as I could.

"I'll be back!" I shouted. "I gotta take a leak!"

Boy, the fruit could change but the toilets sure didn't.

"Jimminy," I coughed as I let the wooden door slam behind me.

The air was cooler up here for sure. Maybe pears liked it cooler. I looked around, same old grimy shacks, with fruit trees bending under the weight of millions of pounds of pears, pale green and beautiful. If I ever had a farm big enough to have folks working for me, I decided, I was never gonna put up a fence between the folks that pick and the folks that don't. When I had a place of my own, if I had a place of my own, there wouldn't be a fence in sight. Except maybe to keep critters out. If absolutely necessary.

"Gosh-darn son of a gun!" I heard a voice call out.

A girl, skinny and tan with knees scraped and bruised, stumbled out of one of the cabins. She was wearing a flour-sack dress that was too big and her hair was wild and stuck up like a barn cat's. She strutted over to the water pump and worked it like she had a bone to pick with the spring below. I watched as she stuck her face right under the spout and slurped. She swallowed, closing her eyes, droplets scattering off her face. When she opened her eyes they locked with mine.

"Well, whatcha looking at?" she sassed.

I smiled and shook my head. "Nothing," I said.

Over my shoulder I saw another truck pulling up, overloaded and grunting. I wondered what kind of truck might carry Terrance, or Quentin, or Clyde. Or Joe Franklin's sweet son for that matter. Wondered who was in it. Could be anyone. Or maybe they was all knee-deep in blackberries, keeping a lookout for me.

In front of me the girl with the mangy hair had dropped down on the step of the cabin and started picking at the scab on her knee. I hooked my fingers in my pockets and sauntered over to her. I'd been looking for someone like her since we left the Santa Ana Holdsten Peach Orchard. Without asking, I sat next to her. She gave me a look that could fry eggs.

"You're an odd one," she muttered under her breath.

"Yeah," I said, looking down the rows and searching for familiar faces.

Maybe someone I knew would step out one of those doors. Maybe it'd be Clyde. Maybe he'd see me and come running. Clap me on the back and start talking about that warm day when I caught Arlon Mackie's ball. Maybe Quentin would pop out and say *Well, what are the odds of us both being here!* Maybe Joe Franklin's sweet son would come around the bend and ask me how to find Jess and I'd roll my eyes and tell him cabin 29 and that he had a stack of love notes waiting back in Balko. Maybe Rudy and Casey and the rest would come running, too, and tell me they already scouted out a place to play. Maybe Terrance would bound up and give me the hug that he couldn't back at the orchard, and maybe we'd ignore the work that was waiting for us back in our little cabins or out in the fields for just a little longer. Or maybe—

"You gonna say something or cat got your tongue?" the girl with the mangy hair piped up.

Maybe . . .

I crossed my arms on top of my knees and rested my chin on my elbow.

Had to start somewhere.

"You wanna play ball?"

The earth shook a bit and the shutter bugs hummed their evening song as she lifted her scrappy face and let a dazzling smile dance across it.

Author's Note

You might be wondering . . . what is real in this
book?

The short answer is that quite a bit is based on
real life, and quite a bit comes from my own imagi-
nation.

Here's the longer answer:

The Willards are invented, but families like
Gloria's were real.

Gloria's story starts in Balko, Oklahoma, which
is a real place in what is called the "panhandle" of
the state. Both Gloria's town and the state were relatively new in 1936 when this story takes place. White
settlers like Gloria and her family were also relatively

new to the area, which was (and is still) home to the Comanche, Wazhazhe (Osage), and Kiowa tribes. White farmers began flocking to the panhandle in the late nineteenth century in the hopes of staking a claim when the territory eventually became a state. These farmers, including Pa and Gloria's granddad, began plowing up Oklahoma's deep-rooted native grass so they could grow crops like broomcorn and wheat. But broomcorn and wheat were never meant to grow in Oklahoma. With every harvest the native plants that held the soil down became scarcer and scarcer. If a drought hit, there would be nothing to keep the soil from eroding and blowing away into dust. The farmers didn't know it, but they were destroying the very land they depended on.

Then the Great Depression hit in 1929 and plunged the nation into the worst financial crisis anyone had ever seen. Everyone was affected, but families living in southern Plains states like Oklahoma were hit particularly hard when severe droughts finally struck in the early 1930s. The land dried out, and with no native prairie grass to hold it in place, the earth simply blew away into dust. Families like Gloria's endured dust storms of biblical proportions. People would stuff rags under every door and at every window and hold wet rags over their mouths and noses to keep the dust out of their lungs.

Breathing dust regularly was not good for anyone, let alone children. Many people developed an illness called dust pneumonia, which is basically like a very, very bad cough. Not everyone recovered. Little Si is a character of my own invention, but his story was sadly a common one for people living in hard-hit areas.

It's no wonder that so many people packed up and left. They were called Dust Bowl refugees, meaning they were forced to leave home because of the disaster. Most refugees back then—just like now—didn't want to leave home. Heading into the unknown when you don't have a lot of money or food can be dangerous, but many made the difficult choice to leave everything behind and head for "greener pastures," as Pa says. Between 1930 and 1940, about 2.5 million people moved out of the Plains states. Of those, 200,000 went to California.

The arrival of Dust Bowl refugees completely changed the ethnic makeup of the workforce. Just a few years before Gloria gets there, most of the workers on large factory farms would have been Mexican, Filipino, or sometimes Black. But the US government took deliberate action to "make room" for the newly destitute white workers from the Plains states. This meant pushing people of color out.

Major laws were passed to keep workers from

other countries out of places like California. And many people were forcibly deported, including thousands of US citizens, most of Mexican descent. When white workers moved into the same low-wage jobs, they were made to feel that they were superior to the people who had been picking those same crops. Many thought they had nothing in common with the nonwhite workers, and bosses did their best to exploit this division.

The newly arrived migrants also faced discrimination. At one point, California actually shut down its own state line to prevent families like the Willards from crossing the border. Californians called the Dust Bowl refugees Okies. Today, descendants of these migrant workers use the term with pride, but at the time, it was a hurtful thing to say and it implied you were ignorant and low-class.

The Santa Ana Holdsten Peach Orchard is my own invention, but places like it were very, very real. Even though America had a federal minimum wage of twenty-five cents an hour, very few farms (if any) actually paid that rate. There were so many people looking for work that the bosses could often get away with paying next to nothing.

On top of that, many "factory farms" pulled every string they could to make sure any money they paid came right back into their own pockets.

Some places required laborers to pay for rent and electricity. Many farms had company stores where they charged outrageous prices. People were tired and hungry at the end of the day, and often bought overpriced groceries on-site rather than having to travel to get cheaper food. Sometimes the farm owners would even hire men to set up card games right outside of where they were paying wages. People desperate for a chance to win a little more money at cards would often gamble their paycheck away before they could even bring it home. As a result, the bosses got to keep a significant portion of money that should have ended up in the pockets of the people picking their crops.

More than a few people thought this was unfair. Factory farms saw numerous strikes like the one Pa tries to lead. Some of these strikes were isolated protests, but many of them were part of a larger effort to unionize farmworkers. Unions are groups of workers who stick together to demand better wages and safer working conditions.

However, it would have been very rare for an average picker like Pa to just up and organize a strike, so that is a bit of fiction on my part. Many of these strikes were led by what the man in the white hat calls "outside agitators." Some of them were union leaders. Some of them were members of the

Communist Party. Some of them were both. They were often called Reds, for a color that has long been associated with workers' rights. They would pose as laborers to get access to the camps and coordinate walkouts and strikes from there. Jimmy's Pa and Grady are those "outside agitators."

Just like in the book, organizing workers was hard and dangerous work. The bosses of factory farms also got together to make sure they could keep paying low wages. Sometimes this meant working with local law enforcement to intimidate people, just like they do at Santa Ana. Sometimes it meant hiring their own muscle to keep people in line. Sometimes it meant offering a few laborers higher wages in return for reporting on "radical activity," just like Sam Blight does. It didn't help that many California locals were also resentful of the migrant workers. Even private citizens made a point of trying to scare them into submission.

If you're thinking that living during the thirties must have been awfully hard, well, you're probably right. But the fact is, no matter how hard things get, people are more than the worst things that happen to them. It's easy to look through history and distill it down to the best and worst things that have ever happened. But most people don't think of themselves as being in the eye of a storm, or at the center of some major moment in time. Most people want to get through their day, see their friends and family, eat good food, and do the things they love. History is just what's happening in the background when you're in your favorite class at school, sitting with your family at dinner, or even on your way to a secret baseball game between a peach orchard and an apricot grove.

If you're interested in reading more about the Great Depression and stories about kids who lived through it, check out these titles:

Brown, Don. *The Great American Dust Bowl*. Houghton Mifflin Harcourt, 2013.

Curtis, Christopher Paul. *The Mighty Miss Malone*. Wendy Lamb Books, 2012.

Freedman, Russell. *Children of the Great Depression*. Clarion Books, 2005.

Hesse, Karen. *Out of the Dust*. Scholastic Signature, 1997.

Holm, Jennifer L. *Full of Beans*. Random House, 2016.

Marrin, Albert. *Years of Dust*. Dutton's Children's Books, 2009.

Nardo, Don. *Migrant Mother: How a Photograph Defined the Great Depression*. Compass Point Books, 2011.

Partridge, Elizabeth. *This Land Was Made for You and Me: The Life and Songs of Woody Guthrie*. Viking, 2002.

Ryan, Pam Muñoz. *Esperanza Rising*. Scholastic Press, 2000.

Sandler, Martin W. *The Dust Bowl: Through the Lens.* Walker and Company, 2009.

Acknowledgments

Half of this book was written at Vermont College of Fine Arts and the other half during a global pandemic with a new baby. In other words, I wouldn't be here without the support of the following saints and superheroes:

My VCFA teachers, who pushed me as far as I could go in the best way possible:

Varian Johnson for helping me discover that this was much more than a short story.

Linda Urban and Jane Kurtz for getting me to realize that no one can break a window without getting in trouble.

Margaret Bechard for pointing out that Gloria didn't need three sisters, just one.

Amy King for keeping me focused on charging forward in the eleventh hour.

Martine Leavitt for pushing me to the finish line (well, the first finish line!).

David Gill for helping keep the dialect real.

Cynthia Leitich Smith for taking the time to share her knowledge with me.

The incredible people at Curtis Brown, but mostly my agent, Ginger Knowlton, for taking a chance on me and Gloria.

The entire team at Margaret K. McElderry Books:

Justin Chanda for the simple but monumental act of saying "Yes, and."

Karen Wojtyla for letting Gloria hang up her hat and kick off her boots at Margaret McElderry.

Bridget Madsen for keeping us steady and on track during a year that was anything but predictable.

My editor, Alyza Liu, for patience that would put Penelope's to shame and the insight of an oracle.

Greg Stadnyk and Sas Milledge for bringing a

world I've only ever seen in black-and-white into vibrant color.

My incredible readers for helping me make this book as authentic as possible:

Kevin Theis for the baseball insight.

Kathryn Olmstead for the history lesson.

Erin Nuttall for telling me that one does not simply climb a peach tree.

Annika M. Prachand, Elaine Pytel, Jonas Gray, and Isla Nuttall for giving me kid insight. No adult in the world could have shared the same wisdom.

My wonderful VCFA classmates, but particularly my Borderless Space Disco Authors, the Turth Machine (no, that's not a typo), and the Sticky Note Group.

All the Chicago theater-makers I've had the pleasure of working with, for teaching me so much about blocking, dialogue, pacing, and stakes.

IATSE for taking care of us during COVID and for the health care that every American deserves.

And finally, my family:

Grandma for sharing so much about her life on a farm, from the heat of the hayloft to the blossoms on the cherry tree.

Mimi for being a writer in the first place.

My mom, dad, and brother for bringing me food, watching my baby, and cheering me on.

My incredible friend, partner, and husband, Kyle, for granting me space and support to have an artistic life.

Elowen, for being you, you, you.

Skyler Schrempp writes books and makes theater in her hometown, Chicago. She lives in an old drafty house with her husband, Kyle, her daughter, Elowen, and a black cat named Masha. She earned her undergraduate degree at Hampshire College and has an MFA from Vermont College of Fine Arts. When she's not writing you can find her making jam from the berries that grow in her backyard or building a fire in her fireplace (depending on the season). You can visit her at www.skylerschrempp.com.